U
the L

'Caramba la hermesetas!' whispered Cuervo. 'You see who it is?'

'I do indeed,' whispered back the Vixen. 'Jack Green, my deadliest enemy!'

'*My* deadliest enemy!' objected Cuervo.

'He was my deadliest enemy before he was your deadliest enemy,' countered the Vixen.

Cuervo shook his head, refusing to accept it.

'No! Because of that man I go to prison where I have to wear a terrible suit that don't fit me properly.'

'He did me much more damage,' purred the Vixen. 'He defeated me in my previous greatest ever crime. And now he shall pay for it!'

'He don't look like he's got that much money,' said Cuervo.

'With his life,' said the Vixen.

*The following books by Jim Eldridge are also available in
Red Fox (incorporating Beaver Books)*

Bad Boyes
Bad Boyes and the Gangsters
Bogeys, Boils and Belly Buttons
How to Handle Grown Ups
More Ways to Handle Grown Ups
What Grown Ups Say and What They Really Mean
Complete How to Handle Grown Ups (3-in-1)
Peregrine Peabody's Completely Misleading Guide to Sport
Peregrine Peabody's Completely Misleading History of the World
Holidays Survival Guide
The Wobbly Jelly Joke Book
Completely Misleading Guide to School
Uncle Jack and Operation Green
Potts

UNCLE JACK . . .
AND THE
LOCH NOCH MONSTER

by Jim Eldridge

Illustrated by
Ann Johns

RED FOX

A Red Fox Book

Published by Random Century Children's Books
20 Vauxhall Bridge Road, London SW1V 2SA

A division of the Random Century Group
London Melbourne Sydney Auckland
Johannesburg and agencies throughout the world

First published by Red Fox 1991

Text © Jim Eldridge 1991
Illustrations © Ann Johns 1991

The right of Jim Eldridge and Ann Johns to be identified
as the author and illustrator of this work respectively has
been asserted by them, in accordance with the Copyright,
Designs and Patents Act, 1988.

This book is sold subject to the condition that it shall not,
by way of trade or otherwise, be lent, resold, hired out,
or otherwise circulated without the publisher's prior
consent in any form of binding or cover other than that in
which it is published and without a similar condition
including this condition being imposed on the subsequent
purchaser.

Set in Times
Typeset by JH Graphics Ltd, Reading

Printed and bound in Great Britain by
Cox & Wyman Ltd, Reading

ISBN 0 09 992890 6

Contents

Chapter One

As Michael Stevens pointed out to his sister, Kate, after it was all over: there should never have been any trouble at all. It was supposed to be a nice quiet family holiday: two weeks staying with Uncle Angus and Cousin Tammy in their cottage in the Scottish Highlands not far from Loch Noch, a quiet country holiday with their parents, Edward and Elizabeth, and their Uncle Jack. Country walks. Birdwatching. Scottish history. All the things that adults want to do on holiday and tell children are good for them, when all children want is a place with a video arcade and loads of fast food. But, of course, the thing that was different was that Uncle Jack was going with them.

Not that what happened was Uncle Jack's fault, but there was no doubt that Uncle Jack certainly stirred things up. That was Uncle Jack's way, and, as it turned out, a good thing it was.

* * *

Mr Stevens checked the clock on the dashboard of the car.

'Two o'clock,' he announced to everyone. 'We should be at Cousin Angus's cottage in about ten minutes.'

Kate and Michael heaved sighs of relief. It seemed as if the drive up from London to the Highlands of

Scotland had taken at least ten days, even though it had actually only been about twelve hours.

Uncle Jack surveyed the surrounding scenery: the beautiful mountains, the sun shining on the waters of Loch Noch.

'It's going to be great to get away from it all for a week,' he said. 'How many years is it since we've been up here, Elizabeth?'

His sister, Mrs Stevens, sitting in the front of the car and navigating (which was one reason why the journey had taken twelve hours instead of the nine which had been predicted), pondered the question.

'Tammy was just three, so it must be nearly ten years,' she said.

'Didn't you come up for Auntie Maggie's funeral two years ago?' asked Michael.

'I'd rather we didn't talk about that, thank you, Michael,' said his mother. 'This is supposed to be a happy holiday time, we don't want to darken it with talk about funerals. And I'd rather you didn't talk about your poor Auntie Maggie in front of Angus and Tammy.'

'What's Tammy like?' asked Kate, curious about this cousin she'd never seen.

'Well . . . ' began Edward carefully.

'I'm sure she's a perfectly happy normal girl,' said Elizabeth.

'It can't have been easy for her, though,' said Jack. 'Her mother dying like that, and Angus trying to bring her up on his own.'

'You're as bad as Michael,' snapped his sister. 'We will not talk about people dying. We are here to have a happy time, and we will have a happy time whether you like it or not. Is that clear?'

'Here we are,' said Edward. 'Angus's place.'

And he turned the car in through an open gateway and pulled up outside a small cottage all on its own amidst the splendour of the mountains. The family eased themselves out of the car and spent the first few minutes straightening up, their knees almost creaking from being cramped in the car. Uncle Jack looked towards the cottage.

'No sign of Angus,' he commented. 'They do know we're coming, don't they?'

'Of course,' said Elizabeth. 'Edward wrote to them.' Then a terrible thought crossed her mind and she turned on her husband accusingly. 'You did write to them, didn't you?'

'Of course I did!' protested Edward. 'Honestly, Elizabeth, sometimes I think that half the time you think I'm an idiot.'

Only half? reflected Jack wryly, knowing how his sister blamed Edward for most of the problems that seemed to occur.

'Maybe they didn't hear us arrive,' said Jack, and he led the way towards the cottage.

Inside the kitchen that was the heart of the cottage all was quiet and empty. There was a half-eaten sandwich on the table. It was as if someone had been disturbed in the middle of a snack and had disappeared.

'Angus!' called Jack.

The family stood and listened, but there was no reply.

'Tammy!' called Elizabeth.

The next second a plastic plate appeared as if from nowhere and smacked Edward on the head.

'Ouch!' went Edward.

Kate and Michael exchanged looks.

'Poltergeists,' said Kate.

Another object suddenly appeared from a cupboard in one corner, this one a cup that narrowly missed Elizabeth.

'Good heavens!' said Elizabeth, alarmed.

Then came a voice from the cupboard, a girl's voice:

'Get outa ma hoose! Ye're nae ganna take me tae nae hame!'

Michael turned to Kate with a grimace.

'We're going to need subtitles while we're up here,' he said.

'Tammy? Is that you?' said Jack. 'This is your Uncle Jack!'

There was a pause, then the figure hiding in the cupboard called out: 'Who?'

The family exchanged puzzled looks. This wasn't the reception they'd expected.

'Are you *sure* you wrote about us coming?' whispered Elizabeth to Edward.

Jack was still talking as he moved cautiously towards the cupboard.

'Remember? We've come to stay with you and your dad for a fortnight's holiday. Your Uncle Edward wrote your dad a letter.'

There was a pause, then the cupboard door opened wider and a small girl of about twelve appeared and looked suspiciously at the family. She scowled at them as they smiled at her.

'I thought ye were the people come tae take me tae the hame,' she said aggressively.

'Why should anyone want to take you to a home?' asked Edward.

'Because ma dad's run off, that's why,' said Tammy, almost defiantly.

'Run off?' said Kate.

Jack and his sister exchanged glances.

'Oh dear,' she whispered. 'I thought that Angus had given up that sort of thing.'

'So did I,' said Jack ruefully. He remembered that his cousin Angus had always been a bit wild, a bit of a wanderer, sometimes going off for days at a time, but he'd thought that since Maggie had died and Angus had Tammy to look after he'd have changed. Gently Jack turned to Tammy. 'What exactly happened?' he asked.

His gentleness wasn't returned.

'I just told ye, he's gone off!' snapped back Tammy rudely. 'Are ye deaf or just plain stupid?'

'Flattery certainly isn't her strong point,' Michael whispered to Kate.

'Tammy. . . ' began Elizabeth gently.

It didn't work.

'Who are you?' demanded Tammy aggressively.

'I'm your Aunt Elizabeth, your father's cousin,' explained Elizabeth. 'We haven't seen each other since you were very small.'

'Huh!' snorted Tammy. 'You don't look anything like ma dad. *He's* good looking.'

'Oh yeah?' snapped Michael, determined not to let this miserable-looking girl continue to get away with insulting his family. 'Well you're not so hot yourself. I've seen better-looking cod.'

'Why you. . . !' began Tammy, and threw herself at Michael, but was grabbed by Jack.

'Hold it! Hold it!' said Jack. 'That was uncalled for, Michael. Look, Tammy, how long is it since your dad went off?'

'Two days ago. He said he was goin' fishin'.'

'Have you been in touch with the police?'

Tammy shook her head.

'No. I didnae want tae get him into trouble.'

'Or yourself taken into a home,' said Jack. 'Right, well that's the answer. Tammy and I will go to the police station and find out if there's been any news of him.'

'No!' said Tammy vehemently. 'I dinna want the police brought intae this.'

'Suit yourself,' said Jack pleasantly, 'but he's my cousin and I'm worried about him, so *I'm* going.'

And with that Jack headed for the door.

'Wait!' called Tammy, and as Jack turned she said sulkily, 'Verra well. I'm comin' wi' ye. He's my dad.'

'Right,' said Michael. 'If she's going so are we. Right, Kate?'

'Right,' said Kate.

And so it was that fifteen minutes later Jack, Kate, Michael and Tammy had parked the car and were walking through the streets of the nearby small town, on their way to the police station. They were nearly there when a sudden cry of 'Help' stopped them in their tracks.

They turned, and saw that a man had just snatched the purse from the shopping basket of an old woman, and was now running off down the street.

'Stay here!' snapped Jack, and the next second he was off in hot pursuit of the thief, running as fast as he could.

'Help!' yelled the old lady. 'That man stole my purse!'

The bystanders nearby looked round to see who she meant. Jack had only got a few metres past the old lady, when suddenly a large man leapt upon him clearly thinking he was the thief, and brought him crashing to the pavement, and three other passers-by then threw themselves upon the fallen Jack, while someone else went off to get the police.

Kate and Michael looked at each other and groaned. It was always the way when they were out with Uncle Jack, *something* awful always happened.

'You'd better stay with Uncle Jack, Kate, and explain who he is,' said Michael decisively taking command. 'Look after him! I'm going after the thief!'

And then Michael set off at a run in the direction the thief had taken, with Tammy following close behind him.

Chapter Two

Police Constable McHugh was fairly new to the force and so he was bursting with pride as he ushered the purse-snatcher he had just arrested in to the police station. You could tell this was a criminal type, he reflected, just by looking at his eyes.

Jack, for his part, held up his handcuffed hands and protested.

'But I tell you I didn't do anything. . . !' he said.

'That's what they all say,' said PC McHugh, and he pushed Jack towards the desk where the Station Sergeant stood, pen poised ready to take down details.

Kate, who had followed them into the station, felt it was time to add her voice.

'He *didn't* do anything,' she insisted. 'I should know, he's our uncle. He was trying to help.'

The Sergeant looked at Kate and frowned thoughtfully, then looked at Jack.

'So you're this little girl's uncle, eh?' he said.

'That's right,' nodded Jack.

The Sergeant's lip curled in a sneer.

'That is despicable,' he said. 'Getting children involved in a life of crime.'

'We weren't involved!' protested Kate. 'He was chasing after the man who did it.'

'Absolutely!' added Jack.

PC McHugh was determined that his first arrest wasn't going to slip away from him as easily as that. He turned to the old lady whose purse had been snatched, while pointing dramatically at Jack.

'Is this or is this not the man. . . ?' demanded PC McHugh.

The old lady peered at the unfortunate Jack through her bottle-thick spectacles. Great, groaned Jack inwardly, trust me to help the very short-sighted.

'It all happened so quickly . . .' said the old lady, doubtfully.

There was a sudden commotion at the door and they all turned round, just in time to see a second constable ushering in the handcuffed figure of the real purse-snatcher, with Michael and Tammy following closely behind.

'We caught him, Uncle Jack!' shouted Michael triumphantly.

'Aye!' added Tammy, pointing at the short-sighted old lady. 'That's the lady! That old bag there!'

'Tammy!' said Jack reprovingly, shocked.

The Sergeant and poor PC McHugh exchanged bewildered looks, as the newly arrived constable took a purse from his pocket and showed it to the old lady.

'Is this your purse, madam?' he asked.

The old lady took the purse, opened it and peered inside, then gave a delighted shout of: 'Yes, it is!'

The Sergeant felt it was about time he got to the bottom of this. He cleared his throat, then demanded: 'All right, what's going on?'

The second constable pointed at Michael and Tammy.

'These two children here called my attention to this character and said they'd been following him as a suspected purse-snatcher. I apprehended him and found this purse in his possession.'

The thief scowled at Michael and Tammy, while the Sergeant looked first at Jack, then at PC McHugh, then back at Jack.

'But if he's the purse-snatcher. . . ?' he began, stunned.

'Exactly,' said the relieved Jack.

The Sergeant glared at PC McHugh.

'McHugh!' he roared.

'Sir?' asked PC McHugh, querulously, although he could see what was coming.

'Get those handcuffs off this man immediately! Then take this lady to the interview room and get a statement from her. You are an incompetent idiot. . . !'

'But, Father . . .'

'And don't call me Father when we're on duty.'

'No, Father,' said PC McHugh sadly, and unlocked the handcuffs from Jack's wrists, all thoughts of promotion and medals vanishing.

The Sergeant turned to the other constable, still holding on to the purse-snatcher.

'As for him, take him through and book him.'

'Right, Uncle,' said the second constable, and dutifully left, taking the thief with him. The Sergeant turned to Jack, a look of deep apology on his face.

'I must apologize for the incompetence of one of my staff . . .' he began.

Jack shrugged the incident aside with a smile.

'That's all right,' he said. 'Thanks to the children the real villain's been caught.'

'If there's anything I can do for ye . . .' persisted the Sergeant, keen to be seen to make amends.

'Actually there is,' said Jack.

'Oh?' said the Sergeant, immediately wary.

'We were on our way to see you, in fact, about my

cousin, Angus McIntosh,' explained Jack. 'He went fishing on the loch a couple of days ago and hasn't been home since. This is his daughter, Tammy.'

The Sergeant smiled down at Tammy, who scowled back.

'Angus McIntosh?' mused the Sergeant thoughtfully, and then he gave a chuckle. 'Oh, aye! He was always doin' that, was Angus, goin' off fer days at a time. That often happens up here, ye ken. Why, my ain grandfather went doon tae the shop tae get some screws for a chair I was making, and it was three months before we saw him again.'

Kate and Michael gaped at him.

'Three months!' said Kate, shocked.

'What did you do?' asked Michael.

'I used nails instead.' said the Sergeant.

'I think they mean about your grandfather,' said Jack.

'Oh, nothing,' said the Sergeant dismissively. 'We knew he'd turn up. Like Angus.' And he winked at Jack and whispered to him, 'He was always a bit of a rover, was Angus.'

'I know,' whispered Jack back, careful to keep his voice down for Tammy's sake, 'but that was before his wife, Maggie, died. Since he's had to look after Tammy on his own he's been more responsible.'

'Mebbe,' whispered back the Sergeant, but he didn't seem too convinced. Aloud, for the benefit of the listening children, he said: 'Two days ago, ye say? Well there's been nae signs of any wreckage or anything being washed up from the loch, but I'll ask people tae keep their eyes oot for him. However, like I say, it wouldnae surprise me to find he just turns up. Ye know Angus.'

Outside the police station Jack and the three children stopped on the steps to hold a council of war.

'The police didn't seem very worried, Uncle Jack,' commented Kate.

'No,' agreed Jack unhappily, 'they didn't.'

'That's because they're idiots!' snorted Tammy. 'They havenae got a brain between them.'

'Are you always this rude about people?' Jack asked her, not really sure if Tammy was really the sort of niece he was happy to admit being related to.

'I think in this case she may be right,' said Michael.

'Who asked you, bignose?' demanded Tammy aggressively, obviously not caring for Michael's show of support.'

'Bignose?' said Michael, stung. 'Why don't you go and play in the road, carrothead?'

'Now, now, that's enough of that!' said Jack, hastily moving between the two of them. 'After all, we are outside a police station. We don't want you two arrested for creating a disturbance.' A sudden thought struck him. 'Tammy, does your father always launch his boat from the same place?'

'Aye,' said Tammy. 'So?'

'Then how about showing us where that is before we go back to the cottage. Who knows, we may be able to find some clues as to where he's gone.'

* * *

The spot at the edge of Loch Noch from where Angus had always launched his boat was covered in woodland, tall pine trees reaching right down to the water's edge. Jack and the three children were following Tammy, crackling their way through undergrowth.

22

'It's just doon here, through these trees,' said Tammy.

Then suddenly their way was barred by a tall wire fence made from very new wire, with barbed wire at the top. Attached to the fence was a wooden board with a large notice on it: 'McLOG MARINE RESEARCH BASE. PRIVATE. KEEP OUT.'

They were just studying the fence and the notice, when a large surly-looking man appeared through the trees on the other side of the fence, glared at them and snapped: 'Oot!'

Jack looked at the man, puzzled.

'I beg your pardon?' he said politely.

'Can ye nae read!' growled the man. 'This is private property! Get oot!'

Tammy glared back at the man.

'This fence wasnae here two days ago!' she snapped.

'Well it's here noo, so get oot!' said the man.

Jack felt it was time to bring some politeness back into the conversation.

'We're looking for a Mr McIntosh. . . ' he began.

'Never heard of him,' said the man quickly.

Jack persisted: 'He launched his fishing boat from here two days ago and hasn't been seen since.'

'There's been nae sign of anybody with a fishing boat,' said the man stubbornly.

'Are ye calling me a liar, fishface?' demanded Tammy, angrily.

'Listen, you horrible child. . . !' began the man.

Although Jack privately agreed with the man that Tammy did appear to be a horrible child, he felt that this arguing wasn't getting them any closer to finding Angus.

'Mr McIntosh always launched his boat from around here,' he said.

'That may well be,' replied the man curtly, 'but that would be before the fence went up. He's nae here now. Now leave before I call for assistance and have ye forcibly removed.'

'But. . .' began Kate, determined to throw her penny's worth in.

Jack laid a hand on her shoulder.

'Come on, children,' he said. 'I think we ought to do as the man says, and leave. I don't want you getting into any trouble.'

As they walked away, Tammy fumed, 'That man's lying!'

Jack nodded.

'Yes, Tammy,' he said. 'I think he is, and I think we have to find out what's really going on.'

Chapter Three

In fact, right at that very moment in the small town where Jack had been arrested as a suspected purse-snatcher, two other people had just arrived who were also intent on finding out just what was going on at the McLog Marine Research Base. They were none other than the Head of MI5, known to his friends (and, indeed, his enemies) as M, and Dorothy Greckle, MI5's Agent 7.

If Jack, Kate and Michael had known of their arrival then maybe things would have happened a lot quicker, because Jack and his niece and nephew were old friends of the British spy pair, having worked with them on a previous case.*

Dorothy opened the creaking door that led into the cobweb-covered Scottish offices of MI5, and looked round at the layers of dust that covered everything. On one wall there was a poster urging all people in the office to keep their mouths shut 'in case the Boers have spies outside the door.'

Dorothy frowned. The Boers? Weren't they the South Africans in 1800 and something?

M came into the room after her, carrying his bulging briefcase.

'Right, Agent 7,' he said briskly. 'Let's get on.'

*See UNCLE JACK AND OPERATION GREEN

26

'If you don't mind me saying so, sir,' said Dorothy, 'this office doesn't appear to have been used a lot.'

'Fortunately we haven't been at war with Scotland for some years,' said M shortly. He blew the dust off the large desk and then unrolled a map on it. 'Right, let us get started Agent 7. We are here to investigate why a company like the McLog Waste Disposal Company are *really* setting up a research base by the side of the loch.'

'They say they're looking for the Loch Noch monster, sir,' said Dorothy.

M heaved a heavy sigh. He sometimes wondered if he had been right to keep Agent 7 on after some of the fiascos she had been involved in. Was she really cut out to be a secret agent? Patiently he explained to her:

'I know that's what they *say* they're doing, Agent 7. But, as I've told you before, people do not always tell the truth. If they did we would be out of work.'

'Yes, sir,' said Dorothy. A thought came to her. 'Sir?'

'Yes, Agent 7?'

'What plans do we have in case *we* should meet the Loch Noch monster?'

M held another heartfelt sigh in check.

'The Loch Noch monster is a myth,' he said, not wanting to destroy all her illusions. After all, it had been only last Christmas the poor woman had found out the truth about Santa Claus.

'A myth?' said Dorothy, puzzled. She hadn't realized that M spoke with a lisp. 'As opposed to a mithter or a mithith?'

M groaned. 'It doesn't exist,' he said. 'Now, can we get on?' He tapped the map on the desk in front of them. 'Let us recap on what we know already. Reports have come in that *someone* has been dumping large amounts of toxic chemical waste here in the open sea near the entrance to the loch.'

'Check,' said Dorothy.

'The toxic waste has gone back into the loch and has mixed together to form a terrible cocktail of chemicals that contaminates living things.'

'Check,' said Dorothy again.

'Do you *have* to keep saying "check", Agent 7?' asked the irritated M.

'Check mate?' suggested Dorothy.

M, deciding to ignore her, continued with the briefing: 'There is a serious danger of those living things being turned into terrible toxic monsters. So, what are the McLog Company really up to? If we assume they were responsible for the dumping, are they goodies or are they baddies?'

'Oh baddies, definitely, sir,' said Dorothy. There was no doubt at all in her mind about that. Anyone who did such a terrible thing was obviously a baddie.

M was not so sure.

'That depends on whether it was an accident, or whether they did it on purpose for some sinister motive. And that, Agent 7, is what we are here to find out.'

* * *

Next morning at the cottage the family were all sitting down to breakfast. All, that is, except Jack, who had announced his intention to go off for an early morning walk, and Edward, who had gone off to fetch some milk.

At one stage it looked as if the situation at the table was going to degenerate into open warfare. Tammy decided to insult Michael and Kate, who immediately

28

responded in kind, and words like 'Pigeonface!' and 'Buckethead!' were bandied about over the cornflakes. In the hope of creating a truce, Elizabeth switched on the radio, and the conversation at the table stopped as they heard the announcer say: 'Special news for all fans of our very own Loch Noch monster. Current activity at the lochside turns out to be a survey by the McLog Marine Research Company into whether or not our own Loch Noch monster actually exists — and the big question is, if it does, will they be able to get a picture of him, her or them? Stay tuned to this station for further updates. And now, especially for Nochie herself — a record: "Monster Mash".'

Preferring classical music herself, Elizabeth switched the radio off, to protests from the children. They were all arguing over whether the radio should be on or off, when the door opened and Jack breezed in, looking very pleased with himself, even though he appeared to have bits of bushes and twigs sticking to different parts of his clothes and poking out of his hair.

'Good morning all!' he greeted them.

'You were up early this morning, Uncle Jack,' said Kate, glad to have someone to talk to who didn't either tell you off (like Mum and Dad) or make fun of you (like Tammy).

'I thought an early morning walk in the country would do me good,' said Jack.

'It looks as if you've brought most of it back with you,' said Elizabeth disapprovingly.

'I had a small accident while climbing a tree,' said Jack.

'Did you go to the loch?' asked Michael, suddenly interested.

'I did indeed,' said Jack.

'We've just been hearing about it on the radio,' said Kate.

Jack looked at them stunned.

'What, me going to the loch?' he asked them in surprise.

'No,' said Michael. 'The loch. They say they're looking for the Loch Noch monster.'

'And so much for your "sinister goings on",' said Elizabeth triumphantly, happy to finish a conversation they had had the previous evening when Jack had outlined his suspicions about 'something sinister going on down by that loch.'

Jack shook his head.

'I still think there's more going on there than just a search for a plesiosaurus,' he said.

'A what?' asked Kate, baffled.

Jack explained, 'All the photographs I've seen of the Loch Noch monster suggests it's actually a plesiosaurus — an underwater member of the dinosaur family.'

'But dinosaurs are extinct!' protested Michael through a mouthful of cornflakes.

'Not all,' said Jack. 'Many of their descendants are still around, and every now and then we discover an underwater animal that we thought had been extinct for millions of years.'

Elizabeth gave one of her disapproving sniffs.

'Honestly, filling the kids' heads with nonsense about Loch Noch monsters.'

'If ye ask me ye're all soft in the heid!' snorted Tammy.

'Then I don't know why we don't just pack up and all go home and let you get on with it!' snapped back Michael, fed up with this horrible cousin of his.

31

'I'll tell you why we won't,' said Jack. 'One, because Cousin Angus is still missing. And, two, because of this.'

And Jack pulled a polythene bag from his pocket, and from out of it he took a twig that was covered in eerie-looking growths. He put it on the table, and everyone recoiled from it in disgust. Elizabeth was particularly indignant.

'Get that off the clean table!' she commanded.

'What is it?' asked Kate and Michael, peering closer at the curious object.

'All the trees around the loch near the Research Base are suffering from this,' said Jack. '*This* is why I think there's something sinister going on there.'

At that moment the door opened and Edward came in carrying two cartons of milk, and a large crumpled brown envelope.

'I'm back!' he announced, 'and look what I found on the doorstep.'

Edward put the milk and the envelope down on the table. The envelope was more than just crumpled, it was as if someone had dragged it through mud. On it was written in a scrawl 'TAMMY'. Jack frowned.

'Did you say you found it on the doorstep?'

Edward nodded.

'Just this very second.'

Jack shook his head, puzzled.

'That's odd. It certainly wasn't there when I came in a minute ago.'

By this time Tammy had torn the envelope open and she turned out the contents on the table: a note with the same scribbled handwriting saying 'Stay away from the loch', and a twig like the one Jack had brought in, covered with the same eerie growths.

The family looked at them, stunned.

'Who can it be from?' asked Edward.

'Is it from your dad?' asked Michael.

Tammy shook her head.

'It doesnae look like his writing.'

'Right,' said Jack, suddenly determined. 'We're going to get to the bottom of this. We'll start by finding out what's happened to these twigs. I think they may well be at the root of this mystery.'

'And how do you propose to do that?' demanded Elizabeth.

'By contacting an old scientist friend of mine — Cynthia Birdwood,' said Jack.

'Isn't she that mad professor we met?' asked Kate warily.

'She is not mad,' defended Jack. 'Slightly eccentric, I'll grant you, but a genius at all things scientific.' He put the twig he had collected back into the polythene bag. 'I'm going to send this twig to her and see what she makes of it. With a bit of luck we should soon find out what's really going on at the McLog Research Base.'

Chapter Four

What was actually going on inside the lab at the McLog Marine Research Base the next morning was that two very worried men were examining a fishing boat that had been washed up on the shores of the loch the day before, and was covered in the same eerie growths that had been on the twig Jack had sent off to Professor Cynthia Birdwood.

One of the men, Oscar McLog himself, shook his head sorrowfully.

'I wonder who was in this boat, Robert, and what happened to them?' he murmured.

Robert sighed.

'That'll be one of the great mysteries in life, Mr McLog,' he said. 'Like "Where do all the ballpoint pens go?" As my Granny used tae say: "Oh whare thae beestie cree doo nar a mickle grae." '

'Thank you for that great and undoubtedly useless thought,' said McLog rather acidly. 'In future please spare me your homespun philosophies.'

He cut a thin slice from one of the growths with a scalpel and took it over to a microscope to examine it in greater detail. Robert meanwhile turned his attention to the rows of TV screens and monitoring equipment that made up one wall of this room at the heart of the research base.

'The contamination seems to be growing, Mr McLog,' he reported.

'Of course it's growing, ye great haddock!' said McLog impatiently. 'We can see that by the stuff on the boat.' He looked into the microscope, then shook his head, deeply worried. 'I tell ye, if the authorities get one whiff of what's gone on here, we're in deep trouble.'

'It wasnae oor fault. . . ' Robert began to protest.

'It wasnae *my* fault!' McLog corrected him. 'It was yours fer using those thin plastic containers to dump the toxic waste.'

'You told me tae get rid of it cheaply!' defended Robert accusingly.

'I didnae know they were going to split like that!' retorted McLog. He groaned. 'And now all that toxic waste has come back intae the loch! We'll get twenty years in prison apiece if the authorities find oot!'

'They won't,' said Robert confidently. 'Ye'll have foond an antidote tae this contamination before they discover anything is wrong.'

'Provided we can stop people from snooping around,' McLog pointed out.

Robert chuckled. 'Aye,' he said, 'that was a brilliant idea of yours, Mr McLog, telling people that we're looking for the Loch Noch monster.' His chuckle turned into a deep-throated laugh. 'The Loch Noch monster indeed! Ha ha ha ha ha ha. . . .'

Suddenly he spotted something on one of the radar screens, and the laugh turned into a sudden hiccup and he sat bolt upright in his chair, his mouth open and his eyes staring.

'Mr McLog!' he gasped. 'Mr McLog!'

McLog carried on looking at the sample under the microscope.

'Dinna bother me,' he snapped irritably. 'Can ye no' see I'm busy.'

'But it's huge.'

McLog looked up, annoyed at his research being interrupted.

'What is?' he demanded.

Robert, still in a state of shock, pointed at the radar screen.

'There! On the screen!'

McLog looked, and his mouth, too, dropped open. There on the screen a huge blob was moving. Something enormous was in the loch, and in the area of contaminated water!

'Good grief!' he said, awed. 'It's . . . it's enormous!'

'Ye know what it is, don't ye!' said Robert. 'It actually exists! It's the Loch Noch Monster!'

Chapter Five

In actual fact the large form moving about underwater in the loch was not the fabled Loch Noch monster, it was a midget submarine. Robert had been partially right, however, because inside the midget submarine were two monsters in human form: one was one of the most evil criminal geniuses ever known, a woman known only as The Vixen; and the other a rather dim but incredibly vicious right-wing Latin American revolutionary in exile, one Generalissimo San Carlos Perdita San Maria Jose Cuervo, known on wanted posters in his home country of San Perdino as simply Jose Cuervo.

The Vixen looked through the lenses of the periscope, peering into the murky waters of the loch, searching for something. Beside her Jose Cuervo practised saluting for when he returned to San Perdino and took power. At the thought his lips curled into a snarl. When that day came, he reflected, then he would have his revenge on those people who insisted on holding such despicable things as elections.

A thought occurred to him, two thoughts, actually, which was a bit of an event for the brain of Jose Cuervo, and he tapped the Vixen on the shoulder.

'Senora Vixen,' he said. 'There are two things I wanna know right now.'

The Vixen moved away from the periscope and looked at Cuervo. Honestly, she thought, of all the idiots I could have chosen, why did I saddle myself with such a complete half-wit as this? Me, a criminal genius!

Cuervo had certainly been surprised when, on his release from prison some three weeks earlier, he had found the Vixen waiting for him in a car outside the prison gates.

'Get in,' she had told him. 'I have a proposition for you which will make you rich and help you get back to power in your country of . . .'

'San Perdino!' Cuervo had cried, his eyes glistening with emotion.

And so the partnership had been agreed. What the Vixen hadn't told Cuervo, however, was his true part in the plan. She liked to have a scapegoat around, so that if ever one of her schemes went wrong she could leave someone else to take the blame while she got clean away. And now her scapegoat had suddenly started to think. How irritating!

'Only two things?' she now enquired, with forced sweetness.

'One,' said Cuervo, holding up one finger, 'what are we a-doing here in a submarine in some Scottish lake?'

'The word is "loch",' said the Vixen, 'and we are here because I have intercepted reports between MI5 and other intelligence agencies of a highly lethal mixture of toxic wastes gathered here. This particular mixture of toxic wastes can create its own life form.'

Cuervo frowned as his brain tried to catch this concept, and missed.

'Its own life form?' he said. 'What is?'

'I think the chemistry might be a bit above you, my dear Generalissimo,' said the Vixen, 'but in layman's terms, when this mixture of chemicals comes into contact with a life form then it can create — all on its own — a deadly toxic monster.' She smiled. 'We are here to help that happen.'

Cuervo nodded, still none the wiser.

'OK. So now I almost know.'

'You said there were two things you wanted to know,' pointed out the Vixen.

'Si,' said Cuervo, and now he put on his Important look, as suited a proper Dictator. 'When do I get to have a go on the periscope? You bin on that periscope all-a the time.'

'Because it is my submarine, and you are working for me.'

Cuervo bridled indignantly at this.

'I ain't-a working for you, I am-a working for the Glorious Revolution which will bring me back to power in my wonderful country of San Perdino,' he said, and then he proceeded to sing his own composition for the new National Anthem of San Perdino, a rendition which was cut short by the Vixen kicking him briskly in the shin.

'For heaven's sake, you're scaring the fishes!' she said.

'You realize you have just kicked the next Presidente of San Perdino,' said Cuervo, much put out.

There was a 'blip' from the sonar, and the Vixen put her finger to her lips.

'Sssh!' she said, and she went swiftly back to the periscope, scanning the murky waters again. Then: 'Ah-ha! Got it!'

'What you got?' asked Cuervo, puzzled.

The Vixen stepped aside from the periscope.

'There! You can look,' she said.

Cuervo moved to the periscope and looked.

'So, it's a fish,' he said, unimpressed. 'What else do you expect to see underwater?'

'Look closer,' said the Vixen.

Cuervo looked closer at the fish.

'Yurk!' he said in disgust. 'It's got-a those things all over it!'

'Exactly!' said the Vixen triumphantly. 'Just like the samples we collected before, but this time they're on a living organism. We shall catch it in the nets and take it back to the laboratory with us.' She smiled a broad smile of evil delight. 'At least we have something living that's contaminated! Now I can create my very own toxic monster!'

'*Our* toxic monster. We are in this together, remember,' Cuervo reminded her sharply.

The Vixen looked at him and smiled.

'Of course, my dear Generalissimo,' she purred, almost cat-like. 'And when this is over you will most certainly get what you deserve, believe me.'

And as she fingered the razor sharp boomerang that she kept on a chain as a necklace, and she smiled again to herself.

Chapter Six

Back at the McLog Marine Research Base, realization suddenly dawned on Oscar McLog as the large blip moved off the radar screen and then disappeared.

'That's no monster!' he cried. 'Listen to that sonar! That thing is made of metal! It's a submarine!'

'I wonder who it was?' wondered Robert.

Before they could discuss the matter further, the phone on the desk rang and McLog picked it up.

'Hello?' he said. He listened for a brief moment, then turned to Robert. 'Do you know a Jack Green, Robert? Janice says he's on the phone.'

Robert shook his head. McLog turned back to the phone.

'OK, Janice, put him on.' There was a click as Janice connected the call, then: 'Good-day to ye, Mr Green. Oscar McLog speaking. What can I do for ye?'

At the cottage Jack weighed up what to say. There was always the direct question, of course: I'm looking for my cousin, Angus McIntosh, have you seen him or his boat? But from the way that the man they'd met at the base had responded to that kind of question, it didn't seem like a good idea. Instead Jack decided to try the subtle approach.

'Good day to you, Mr McLog,' he said. 'My name's Jack Green. You may have heard of me. I write books and articles about environmental issues. At the moment

I'm writing an article about the pollution of the Scottish Lochs and, in view of the work you're doing at the moment on Loch Noch, I'd like to talk to you.'

If Jack expected a welcoming response, or even a cautiously welcoming reponse, he was sadly mistaken. McLog's answer was brief and to the point,

'This area's out of bounds tae everyone. Any trespassers coming here will be shot. Goodbye.'

And with that there was a loud click in Jack's ear as McLog hung up.

Jack replaced the phone with a rueful grin. 'Not exactly my most successful approach,' he said to himself. 'But to my mind it certainly proves they're hiding something.'

A crash from Tammy's bedroom upstairs, followed by the sounds of Tammy and Michael arguing, made Jack look up.

'Me? Being horrible?' Jack heard Michael demand indignantly.

'Aye!' shouted back Tammy. 'Horrible, horrible, horrible! And ye've got a face like a bucket of sick!'

'Well you're the most horrible person I've ever met in the whole universe!' retorted Michael loudly. 'And I expect if we ever went to any other universe you'd *still* be the most horrible person there is!'

By this time Jack had made it to the top of the stairs and had opened the door of Tammy's room, where Kate, Michael and Tammy stood and shouted at each other. A nice quiet family holiday in the country, he groaned quietly to himself. Aloud, he said:

'All right, you three, what's going on?'

The three children all started to talk at once.

'She said. . . !'

'Tammy said to Michael . . .'

'This eejit. . . !'

'One at a time,' said Jack. 'Tammy.'

'He said ma dad wasnae coming back fer forty years!' shouted Tammy with great fury.

'No I didn't!' protested Michael. 'All I said was maybe Uncle Angus had lost his memory, and I said I'd seen on TV about a man who lost his memory for forty years. That was all.'

'And then he said I'd be over fifty when Dad came back, and think of the pocket money he'd owe me,' added Tammy, still fuming.

'I was only trying to cheer her up! And then she started throwing things.'

Tammy was just about to pick up something else and throw it, when there was a knock at the door downstairs.

'That may be aboot ma dad!' said Tammy, and next second she was out of the door and downstairs, with Jack, Kate and Michael close behind her.

Expectantly Tammy wrenched open the front door, and there, standing on the doorstep was a perky lady in her late fifties, with two enormous suitcases next to her. Behind her a taxi was just driving off.

'Who are ye?' demanded Tammy aggressively.

'I'll tell you who she is,' said Jack. 'It's my friend Professor Birdwood. Hello Cynthia. What are you doing here? I only sent you something yesterday.'

But he was addressing an empty doorway. Cynthia Birdwood had already swept into the kitchen and was sizing it up.

'Unload the first suitcase and get my laboratory equipment set up on this table,' she commanded. 'The second suitcase can go up to my room.'

The others exchanged puzzled looks.

'But . . .' began Jack, hoping for some kind of explanation.

'What are you still all standing there for?' demanded Cynthia. 'There's no time to waste! That twig you sent me! It's a catastrophe! Come on, give me a hand to get my stuff in! We've got important work to do!'

* * *

Meanwhile, at the small sub-office of MI5 in the nearby town, M and Agent 7 were examining a map of the McLog Marine Research Base.

'What we are going to do,' announced M importantly, 'is get in there and find out what is really going on.'

Dorothy nodded

'You know who we need on this case, don't you sir?' she said thoughtfully. 'That green man, sir. Jack Green. Remember he helped us before on the case of the poisoned gas, when we beat that arch-criminal, The Vixen. I'm sure Jack Green could get to the bottom of this. After all he is an expert on environmental pollution, and getting things put right.'

M looked coldly at Dorothy.

'Nonsense, Agent 7,' he said. 'For one thing the man is hundreds of miles away in the South of England. For another, he may be very well-meaning but he is an amateur. This is a job for the professionals.'

'But, sir . . .'

'There are no "buts", Agent 7. During that last escapade when we were involved with this man Green, I noticed that you developed a soft spot for him, didn't you.'

'Me, sir? Oh gosh, no, sir,' protested Dorothy.

46

'Don't try to pull the wool over my eyes. I am a trained investigator. I know a soft spot when I see one. Well let me give you some advice. In this world of international espionage, crime and corruption there is no room for soft spots. We are hard people, Agent 7. Tough. We do not have soft spots. We do not have spots of any sort.'

'Agent 21 does, sir,' Dorothy pointed out. 'Terrible big spots and pimples. His code name in Washington is Agent Zit.'

'I'm talking about *inner* spots.'

'He's got those as well, sir. Mouth ulcers.'

'You must learn to be ruthless, Agent 7. Totally without ruth. There is no room for sentiment in our world.'

'Right, sir,' agreed Dorothy, but feeling that Sir was missing out on an awful lot of fun if that was how he really felt. M, meanwhile, had got up and was pacing around the office as he outlined his new daring plan.

'We have to get inside this research base. And I intend to do that *myself*, disguised as a bagpipe mender. Brilliant, eh, Agent 7?'

Dorothy regarded him, a doubtful expression on her face.

'What about the Scottish accent, sir?' she asked. 'Not that I'm suggesting . . .'

'That is the brilliance of this scheme,' M interrupted her. 'P has sent me up this.' And here M produced a tiny device that looked like a miniature battery for a digital watch. Dorothy looked at M, puzzled.

'Pee?' she said.

'The person in charge of new inventions,' said M.

'I thought that was Q,' said Dorothy.

'It used to be Q but he retired, so now we've got P. P comes after Q.'

Dorothy shook her head: 'P comes before Q. A B C D . . .'

'Normally, Agent 7, yes, but that is the other brilliant touch in this case. We're working backwards!'

Dorothy looked at him.

'Gee!' she said.

'Not "G", 7. P.'

'I didn't mean "Gee" as in "G", sir, I meant "Gee" as in "Gosh".'

'What on earth are you blathering about, Agent 7? Can we get back to this invention? The way it works is this: I set it to any accent I wish, in this case Scots; place it in my mouth, and then . . .'

And with that M put the tiny metal disc into his mouth and began to speak, and it was as if the great Scottish poet Robert Burns himself had returned and was delivering one of his unintelligible poems.

'Gosh, sir!' said Dorothy, impressed. 'That is terrific!'

Her look of awe and astonishment vanished, however, as M suddenly started speaking in a Chinese dialect.

'If you don't mind me saying so, sir,' she said, 'that doesn't sound very Scottish.'

M took the small metal gadget out of his mouth and frowned at it.

'A minor problem obviously caused by a short circuit from the metal fillings in my teeth. But it will work perfectly when it needs to, Agent 7. Your role in this adventure is to act as my back-up. Follow me and make sure that I am not followed.'

'Who by, sir?'

'Anyone. We must take no chances. These may be very dangerous people we are up against.'

* * *

Although M didn't know it, right at that very moment two very dangerous people were just stepping down from the escape hatch of their midget submarine into the laboratory that the Vixen had constructed inside a huge cave.

The Vixen delicately carried the polythene bag containing the contaminated fish they had taken from the waters of the loch. Behind her came Jose Cuervo, looking around him and still impressed by all the scientific apparatus. This Vixen, he reflected, she is some real clever woman. Often he asked himself, what is she up to with all this? And every time back came the answer: I dunno.

As they stepped into the large area of the cave that the Vixen had transformed into what looked like an operating theatre, complete with an operating table in the centre, he commented: 'I still don't-a see what's so good about what we just done. It's just a fish.'

'That, my dear Generalissimo Cuervo,' said the Vixen with a sweet smile, 'is because you have the brain of an idiot chicken.'

Cuervo looked indignant.

'Hey! No "chicken!" I, Generalissimo Jose Cuervo, am a lion!'

'Very well, you have the brain of an idiot lion.'

Cuervo nodded.

'That's better,' he said. 'But what we gonna do with this fish?'

The Vixen hung the polythene bag containing the fish on a hook.

'Simple,' she said. 'Using the contaminated cells from this fish, I am going to create a living monster that will spread fear and terror throughout the world, and once I unleash it the world will come to me — us — begging us to stop it. Which we will do — for a price.'

'But not in San Perdino, eh,' insisted Cuervo. 'I will-a take-a this creature to San Perdino and will take back my country with a Glorious Revolution!'

'Of course,' soothed the Vixen.

She strode towards the operating table on which lay a large sheet covering something that looked vaguely human in its shape.

'I have been keeping this part of our operation secret from you because I did not think you were ready. However, I think now is the time for it to be revealed.' With that she pulled off the sheet with a flourish, and revealed what looked like the figure of a human being lying on the operating table, but made entirely out of masses of seaweed. 'There!'

Cuervo looked at it, none the wiser.

'So? It's a load of seaweed and stuff. What are we gonna do — eat it?'

The Vixen resisted the temptation to bash Cuervo over the head, and began patiently to explain the process of her experiment.

'I am going to transplant the cells from that fish into this — as you so blithely call it — mass of seaweed. Now, if my theories are correct, then the combination of those cell, and this . . .'

Suddenly realization hit Cuervo, and his mouth dropped open in shock and admiration.

'The monster! *This* is the monster!'

The Vixen nodded and smiled.

'And it will grow, my dear Generalissimo. My researches so far have shown that this stuff increases in size at an alarming rate. And seaweed multiplies on its own. We are going to have millions and *millions* of monsters! We will be able to hold the whole world to ransom!'

Chapter Seven

Meanwhile, back at the cottage, Professor Cynthia Birdwood had moved in with a vengeance. The once peaceful kitchen had been transformed into something that looked like Frankenstein's laboratory: all bubbling retorts and rows and rows of glass tubes frothing away, filling the house with weird (and sometimes downright unpleasant) smells as Cynthia tested the twig to see if she could isolate the toxic contamination and so find an antidote to it.

The family watched her as she placed a small piece of the contaminated twig in a glass tube and put the tube into a jar filled with bubbling pink liquid.

'Stand back,' she said, and she moved away from the experiment.

'Why?' asked Edward.

There was a phhtttt! from the glass jar, and then the small piece of twig hurtled out of the tube and hit the ceiling with a splat!

'Because of that,' said Cynthia. She sounded disappointed.

'Not going well?' asked Jack, cautiously.

'Oh, well enough,' said Cynthia. 'At least I know why this contamination has happened.'

'Oh?'

'It's a mixture of toxic chemicals and it's actually creating another life form, and a deadly life form at that. A sort of cocktail for making toxic monsters. All I need

to do is identify the cell structure that actually binds them together and then produce an antidote to undo it, and we've cracked it.'

'That's *all*?' echoed Michael in bewilderment.

'Well obviously it's a bit difficult because it's a new substance, self-creating,' said Cynthia. 'One problem is that I haven't got enough of this twig sample left to carry on testing properly.'

'That's not a problem,' said Jack. 'I got that one, I can soon bring back a few more.'

'We're coming with you!' said the three children in a chorus, even Tammy for once joining in.

Jack shook his head.

'You certainly are not. If the area is contaminated as Professor Birdwood says then you're not going anywhere near it.' With that Jack grabbed his coat and headed for the door. 'I won't be long,' he said. He grinned. 'And let's hope I don't bump into any of these toxic monsters you're talking about.'

* * *

Ten minutes later Jack was back in the small wood near the loch, and near the McLog Marine Research Base, looking up at the trees and deciding which of the contaminated twigs he would take back to Cynthia for her experiments.

It was as he was looking up at the trees that he began to feel as if someone was watching him. Perhaps it was that man again, the one who had ordered them away from the fence so rudely?

Jack looked round. There didn't seem to be anyone there. Strange, though, he definitely had a feeling of being watched. He shrugged and turned back to looking up at the branches of the contaminated trees.

In fact, Jack *was* being watched, and by the strangest of creatures. Hidden in the dense undergrowth not far away from Jack, and creeping ever so slowly nearer and nearer to Jack's back, was a creature that almost defied description: something human-shaped, about two metres tall, and covered with the same eerie growths that were on the twigs that Jack was looking at.

As the creature watched, its eyes glinting in the hideous mass of growths that formed what looked like its face, Jack turned away from the particular tree he was studying and moved deeper into the small wood, away from the staring creature that was watching him. Jack was just passing a clump of bushes when suddenly a human arm popped out from the bushes, bashed Jack on the side of the head with a stick then dropping the stick, hauled him roughly into the bushes.

Chapter Eight

'Jack!'

Jack lay on the floor, stunned and covered in twigs and bits of bush. He looked up, straight into the worried face of Dorothy Greckle.

'Dorothy!' He felt the side of his head where he had been struck and wondered if he could feel a bump starting. 'Was that you who hit me?' he asked, puzzled.

'Er, it was a branch,' lied Dorothy, who had hit him before she recognized her old friend.

She helped him to sit up and began to dust him and pick pieces of undergrowth off him.

'What are you doing here?' asked the bewildered Jack, shocked at seeing Dorothy so far away from MI5's office in London.

'I'm acting as back-up for M. In case anyone should have been following him.'

'M? He's here as well? Where?'

'He's trying to get into the McLog Marine Research Base disguised as a bagpipe mender.'

'So I'm right, there *is* something sinister going on there!' said Jack triumphantly, clambering back to his feet. 'Dorothy, tell me everything you know. My cousin Angus's life is at stake.'

M, meanwhile, was not having a lot of luck at the Marine Research Base. It had started well enough. He had rung the bell in the reception area and a large miserable looking man, who turned out to be Oscar

McLog's First Assistant, one Robert Murray, had appeared and had apparently not so much as twitched an eyebrow as M laid the reason for his calling before him, as a 'bagpipe mender'.

(However, that was only M's opinion. When Robert laid eyes on M, dressed up in kilt, sporran, bonnet, and with a set of bagpipes under his arm, his first reaction was: 'Either this man's an escaped lunatic or a practical joker.')

Robert's worst fears were confirmed as M began to talk. It started off well enough, with M saying in a passable broad Scots accent: 'G'd day tae ye, ma name is Hector McLaird, Master Craftsman bagpipe mender. D'ye ha' any bagpipes that need mendin?' But the effect was ruined, and Robert's suspicions hardened, when the alleged bagpipe mender began talking in what sounded remarkably like Polish.

'That does it!' snapped Robert sharply. 'Oot!'

'Oot?' said M, recovering his Scots accent.

'Aye. Ye're either Jeremy Beadle or Candid Camera, and whichever ye are, unless ye're oot of here in ten seconds, I'm ganna smack ye over the head wi' a shovel.'

M looked at Robert, shocked.

'Ye'd hit a puir bagpipe mender?'

Robert didn't even begin to enter the discussion. 'Ten . . .' he began grimly.

'But . . .' protested M, and then again began to natter away in some unintelligible dialect, this time a form of Serbo-Croat. Curse that idiot, P, and his stupid inventions, he thought vengefully. I'll kill him when this is over.

Robert reached for a shovel, which was leaning against one wall, left there by the builders of the base.

'Three!' he said menacingly.

At this M protested volubly, and luckily in Scots: 'Ye missed oot nine tae fuir!'

'Because I canna bear yer blatherin',' growled Robert, and he picked up the shovel and began to lift it above his head. 'Two.'

'Verra well,' said M with all the dignity he could muster. 'But you are a verra cruel man who deserves to have his bagpipes gae all wonky.'

And with that M bowed, and took his leave.

Outside the base M stood fuming for a second or two, then he took the microscopic metal disc out of his mouth and threw it away from him as hard as he could. Blast P! That was the last of that sort of thing he was going to try out.

M suddenly became aware of Dorothy Greckle approaching him, and with her was none other than — good heavens — Jack Green!

As Jack and Dorothy came up to M, Jack took in the outfit, including the kilt which showed M's very knobbly knees to great effect, and couldn't resist a smile.

'Miss Scotland, I presume?' grinned Jack.

M looked at him stiffly, trying to retain his dignity.

'What are you doing here, Mr Green?' he asked sniffily.

'He says he thinks he knows what's going on,' put in Dorothy.

M looked at Jack suspiciously. Typical, he thought. This amateur poking his nose in things again. What was so annoying was that this man Green so often seemed to succeed where the authorities failed.

'How did you get on, sir?' asked Dorothy.

'A temporary hitch, Agent 7,' said M airily.

'You mean they didn't want their bagpipes mended?' asked Jack.

M bridled. 'You may scoff, Mr Green, but can you do any better?'

Jack thought it over. 'Yes, I think I can,' he said. 'Wait here for me.'

And as M and Dorothy watched, he headed for the base.

Jack's plan was simple. From what he had learned from Dorothy and Cynthia it was obvious that there had been some terrible environmental calamity involving toxic waste, and that the McLog organization was the possible cause of the disaster and all this stuff about searching for the Loch Noch monster was just a cover-up. The proof was the contamination of the twigs, and right now he had a bagful of that proof in his pocket, samples he'd collected to take back to Cynthia. Using that evidence, he intended to force the McLog organization into coming clean with what was going on, and then maybe by doing that they'd get to the bottom of what had really happened to Angus.

Jack entered the reception area of the base and pressed a bell marked 'Visitors, please ring.'

Almost immediately a man appeared, the same grim-faced man who had ordered him away from the fence the day before. Jack greeted him with a smile.

'Good day to you,' he began.

Robert was in no mood to mess about with further visitors, especially not after that idiot who had pretended to be a bagpipe mender. He pointed towards the door.

'Oot!' he ordered. 'No unauthorized people allowed.'

'Oh dear,' said Jack, 'and I have a message for Mr McLog.'

At that moment Oscar McLog himself appeared, curious to know who all these visitors were who'd suddenly taken to arriving. He'd heard Jack's last sentence and asked: 'What sort of message?'

Robert turned to McLog apologetically.

'I'm sorry, Mr McLog, he must've sneaked in. I was just aboot tae throw him oot.'

'And that would be a pity before you had a chance to hear what I've got to say,' said Jack.

McLog regarded Jack suspiciously.

'Who are ye?' he demanded.

'Jack Green,' smiled Jack, determined to keep the thing on a friendly footing. 'We spoke on the telephone this morning . . .'

McLog shook his head. 'I have nothing tae say tae ye. Robert, throw him oot. And see that he injures himself when he lands.'

'Right, Mr McLog,' said Robert, moving towards Jack in a menacing fashion.

Jack moved slightly back from the advancing Robert.

'There's no need for that,' he said pleasantly. 'If that's how you feel, I shall go. And you can read what I have to say in the newspapers.'

At the word 'newspapers' Robert stopped and cast a sharp look at McLog, who had also stopped in his tracks and was now looking at Jack. Newspapers? The thought sent shock waves surging through McLog's body. The last thing they wanted was busybodies from the newspapers snooping around!

Jack had reached the door by this time. He turned and smiled pleasantly at McLog and Robert.

'Good day,' he said.

'Wait!' said McLog.

Jack stopped, framed in the doorway. I thought that would worry them, he thought.

'Yes?' he asked, innocently.

'Why should I be interested in what ye might say in some newspaper?' demanded McLog.

'Because I know what's going on here,' he said.

'Aye!' said Robert quickly. 'We're looking for the Loch Noch monster.'

Jack shook his head. 'I mean, what's *really* going on here.' And Jack took a bag from his pocket, and out of it he took two of the twigs that he had collected.

At the sight of them Robert drew in his breath sharply. McLog glowered and moved menacingly towards Jack.

'I warned ye what I'd do if ye've been trespassing . . .' he growled.

'I didn't need to trespass to collect these,' said Jack. 'I got them from trees outside your fence. Toxic waste contamination, I believe.'

'Rubbish!' snorted McLog defiantly.

Jack smiled.

'Very well, if you prefer, toxic rubbish contamination.'

McLog pointed at the twigs that Jack was holding.

'Those twigs are nothing tae do with us!' he snarled.

'Then you won't mind if I come in and look around and ask you a few questions. Or would you prefer that I wrote my newspaper article without talking to you first?'

McLog and Robert exchanged worried looks, then McLog nodded.

'All right — this afternoon?'

Inwardly Jack heaved a sigh of relief. Great! That would give him time to work out what he should be looking for.

'OK,' he said. 'One o'clock?'

'That'll be fine,' nodded McLog.

'Good,' said Jack, and he put the two contaminated twigs back in the bag, and back in his pocket.

'Where are ye taking those twigs?' demanded Robert, furious.

'Away,' said Jack, adding with a smile, 'After all, they're nothing to do with you, are they? Good day. I'll see you in a couple of hours.'

And with that Jack nodded politely to them, and left.

Right, he thought triumphantly, now I think we've got things moving. Nothing like setting a cat among the pigeons.

Outside the base he found Dorothy and M waiting for him.

'If you've ruined this operation . . .' began M accusingly.

'I don't think so,' said Jack modestly. 'I've been invited to go and look around the base.'

'Oh well done, Jack!' said Dorothy, delighted. 'Isn't he clever, sir! Succeeding where you failed.'

M glared at her. He didn't need reminding. He turned back to Jack.

'Mr Green, I think it might be a good idea if we had a little chat.'

Chapter Nine

Jack, Dorothy and M gathered round M's desk at the MI5 Scottish office and looked at the twig that Jack had placed on it.

'The growths on this twig are the result of toxic wastes combining to form a lethal cocktail which is working on the living cells. My friend Professor Birdwood, identified it as such. The next thing to do is tell the press what is happening. It is important that we let people know what is going on at the base.'

M shook his head.

'I'm afraid we can't do that, Mr Green,' he said.

'But why not?' demanded Jack. 'This contamination could do terrible things! People should know!'

'I'm afraid that's out of the question. We must keep it secret because we don't know why it's happened. We suspect the McLog Waste Disposal Company are behind it, but we don't know if they did it on purpose, or it happened by accident.'

'Why don't you ask them?' demanded Jack.

M laughed, a superior sort of chuckle. 'Ask them? Ha ha ha ha. How naive the general public are . . .'

'It's certainly what I intend to do,' said Jack.

M stared at him, horrified.

'But you can't!'

'Why not?'

'Because if it has been done for some malicious purpose and we confront them direct, all they will do is switch their operation elsewhere. We have to find out why they are doing it, and who's behind them.'

'Then we can stop them doing what they're doing again. For ever. Right, sir?' put in Dorothy.

'Precisely. Are you with us, Mr Green?'

Jack shook his head. 'No. My cousin Angus has already disappeared. Who knows what may be happening to other people. For one thing, why haven't the police been told about this?'

'We don't always think it's a good idea to let the police know what's going on,' said M. 'They're not the most security-minded organization in the world. All that chatting to criminals that goes on. And national security is at stake here.'

'Be blowed to national security!' stormed Jack. 'What about people's safety? This matter should be given to the press. That's certainly what I intend to do!'

'I'm afraid I cannot let you do that,' said M, and there was no mistaking the touch of menace in his voice. 'If you do I shall have to have you locked up as a danger to national security. After all, we can't have you spilling the beans and ruining our chance to stop this terrible thing.'

Dorothy looked at her boss, shocked by this suggestion.

'You can't lock him up, sir!' she protested. 'What about the others?'

'The others?' asked M, puzzled.

'Professor Birdwood. Kate, Michael, Jack's sister and brother-in-law,' Dorothy said, ticking them all off on her fingers. 'They're up here as well and they know all about it.' With a note of triumph in her voice she added: 'You'd have to lock them up, as well!'

M smiled and gave a little nod.

'Yes, I would. Thank you, Agent 7.'

Jack gave Dorothy a rueful look. Poor Dorothy, once again she had put her foot right in it, for him and the whole family.

'Well, Mr Green? Are you with us?' asked M.

Jack shrugged. 'As you've threatened my family, it doesn't seem as if you've left me much choice. Very well. But it you're wrong and I see people suffering because of our silence, I warn you, I shall go public with it, whatever you threaten.'

* * *

Inside the cave that housed the Vixen's laboratory, final preparations were underway to bring the monstrous mass of seaweed to life. The Vixen had connected up electrical cables to the human-shaped mass of seaweed on the operating table, and a plastic tube dripped the contaminated cells from the fish into the heart of the mass.

While the Vixen was at work carrying out the final details, Jose Cuervo stood and admired himself in the chrome of a piece of electrical apparatus.

'Estupendo, hermoso,' he said to himself, 'but you're good-a-looking!'

'Thank you,' replied the Vixen, working with a pair of tweezers on the seaweed.

Cuervo turned and looked at her, puzzled. Then the penny dropped.

'Oh! Si! You as well.' As he looked at her, a thought began to take shape in his head. This Vixen, she was clever, eh? Clever and cruel. They would make a good partnership, one that could rule San Perdino with absolute fear and terror. He nodded to himself. A great idea, and one that he was sure the Vixen would be

attracted by. And why not? After all, he was everything a woman could wish for: handsome, brave, strong, intelligent.

'Hey, Vixen,' he said with a forced casualness. 'You know, you an' me we make-a the pretty good team, eh? Maybe we could make it . . .' and he gave a little smirk, 'permanent?'

The Vixen stopped what she was doing and turned to look at him, open-mouthed.

Permanent? Surely this idiot wasn't seriously thinking that *she* could. . . ?

'Are you proposing to me? Marriage of some sort, I mean?' she demanded, and only Cuervo could have missed the glint of insult in her eye.

'Why not?' said Cuervo with what he took to be a winning smile. 'Back in San Perdino we'd be sitting pretty with what we got. Think about it. I got intelligence, courage, good looks, ambition, an' you know how to cook.'

The Vixen glared at him, her mouth dropping open in indignation.

'Cook?'

'Si. Like-a this seaweed monster. Is-a cooking really, eh?'

The Vixen just stopped herself from picking up the nearest large object and braining Cuervo with it on the spot.

'You incompetent moron! I'll have you know that I have seven Degrees, three Masters and two Doctorates.'

'Two doctors?' said Cuervo, puzzled.

'Do you seriously believe that I would ever, ever, ever consider setting up with you in San Banana. . . ?'

'San Perdino,' Cuervo reminded her, hurt at this insult to his beloved country.

'To waste one of the greatest criminal minds the twentieth century has ever known on you?' continued the Vixen, her ire now raised to the fullest.

'OK, you wouldn't have to cook,' relented Cuervo. 'We could get a microwave . . .'

Unable to express her anger in words any more, the Vixen pointed at a spot on the operating table.

'Place your head there,' she said.

Cuervo smirked. 'Hey, you need-a my help with this experiment, right? See. You need-a me.'

And with that he took off his general's hat and laid his head on the corner of the table.

Smack! With one swift move, the Vixen had snatched up a large, wet, dead fish and bashed Cuervo with it.

'Argh!' yelled Cuervo, staggering back from the table, holding his head.

'I think that answers your question. Now, to business. . . .'

And while Cuervo held his still ringing head in his hands, the Vixen completed the electrical connections to the mass of seaweed and strode over to the generator next to the operating table.

'Now we shall see some action!'

And with that she pressed a button and the generator came into life and electricity began to surge into the mass of seaweed.

Cuervo was not interested in the seaweed. His pride had been hurt. Also his head. He needed a drink of something to get his brain working again after that bash with the fish. He picked up a small plastic cup from a bench and sniffed the liquid. Ah, lemonade! His favourite!

He drank the lemonade, which seemed to him to

have a bit of a funny taste, and watched the Vixen at work as she hovered over the seaweed. To his eye, nothing seemed to be happening, just loads and loads of blue sparks dancing over the mass of green weed.

'You really reckon is-a gonna work, hey? This-a monster?' he asked, determined to forgive her for the assault on his person with the dead fish. After all, he was sure she would come round to his way of thinking in time.

'You forget that I am a criminal genius,' said the Vixen curtly. 'In a few moments more this mass of seaweed will get up and walk, just as soon as I have added the final ingredient!'

And she reached towards the bench, and then stopped.

'Where is it?' she demanded.

Cuervo looked puzzled.

'Where is what?' he asked.

'The final ingredient. It was here in a plastic cup.'

Cuervo looked at the empty plastic cup that he had just thrown in the waste bin.

'What. . . . what was it?' he asked.

'A special preparation made of toad's brain cells,' said the Vixen.

Cuervo clutched his stomach. He was beginning to feel sick.

'And a fish's intestines,' added the Vixen.

Cuervo retched suddenly, and the Vixen glared at him as realization dawned as to what had happened to her magic final ingredient.

'You half-brained idiot!' she raged, and she shut off the generator.

'How was I to know!' protested Cuervo. 'It was in a cup.'

71

'Get back to the submarine!' snapped the Vixen, pointing towards their midget sub. 'That was the last piece of fresh intestine.'

Cuervo looked furious. This was the last straw, this woman telling *him*, Generalissimo Jose Cuervo, what to do.

'Don't-a you tell-a me what to do!' he said, drawing himself up to his full height. 'Remember, I am-a Generalissimo San Carlos Perdita San Maria Jose Cuervo, Saviour of San Perdino and-a Master of-a all I survey!' Out of the corner of his eye he saw the Vixen reaching for the large dead fish again, and he reflected that this was some tough lady. '*I* tell-a me what to do! "Generalissimo Jose Cuervo?" "Si!" "Get in-a the submarine!" "Si, senor! I obey!" '

And with that Cuervo headed for the submarine, the Vixen following him, still fuming that she should have saddled herself with such an incompetent moron as an accomplice.

Chapter Ten

Jack checked his watch. Nearly one o'clock. They were right on time, they should be at the McLog Marine Research Base in about two minutes. Dorothy, who was walking along the path beside Jack, was going to pose as his secretary. Inside her bag was a small tape recorder, and concealed in the brooch on her lapel was a tiny camera, ready to photograph the interior of the base.

Jack glanced back to check that M was still behind them. There he was, half-hidden among the trees. In fact with M's latest camouflage disguise it was difficult to see him properly, because M had now dressed up as some sort of walking bush.

Jack gave M a thumbs-up, then he and Dorothy went through the gates into the Marine Research Base.

In the small wood, M paused and leant against a tree. This was a brilliant disguise, he thought. Definitely the best idea P had had, it more than made up for that ridiculous foreign accents gadget. Why, thought M, I could stand here and no one would notice me. If anyone did come they would just think I was a bush. Like that one over there.

M stopped, shocked. Had that bush over there *really* moved? Surely not! It was obviously imagination. He must have been working too hard lately.

M stepped forward to take a closer look at the bush, and then suddenly saw that it wasn't a bush! Now he was

73

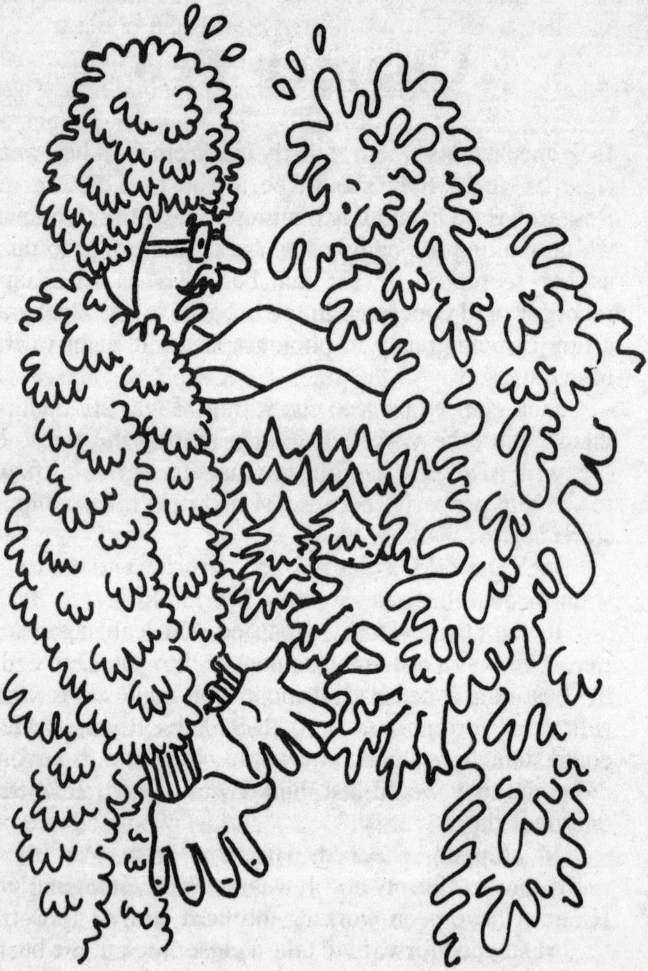

closer, he saw it looked like a man, but it was covered in hideous growths, the same sort of growths that had been on that twig of Jack Green's. It was a monster! A toxic monster! The awful predictions had come true!

Overcome with shock and feelings of horror, M turned to run away before the monster spotted him. That movement was his downfall. The monster caught a glimpse of M moving out of the corner of its eye, and turned towards him.

For a second the two creatures stared at each other: the one human-shaped and covered in hideous growths, its two eyes glinting in a face that was a mass of vegetation; and the other looking like a walking bush. The next second they both threw up their arms, and rushed off, intent on getting as far away from each other as they could, M stumbling and crashing through the undergrowth towards the McLog Marine Base, and the monster running deeper into the woods.

* * *

Inside the Marine Research Base, Jack had begun confidently enough. He sat facing Oscar McLog with his notebook opened and ready to take notes and Dorothy sitting next to him. Robert stood grim-faced behind McLog.

'As I said,' began Jack, 'I'm writing an article about pollution of the Scottish lochs,' and he produced one of the contaminated twigs, 'in particular, this . . .'

McLog smiled, and this gave Jack a feeling of unease. The man seemed suddenly very sure of himself. What had happened in the hours since he had last been here that had given McLog this new air of confidence?

75

'Like I said tae ye before, this is nothing tae do with us,' said McLog. 'We're just here looking for the Loch Noch monster.'

'Have you seen it yet?' asked Dorothy, interested.

'No,' said McLog, while simultaneously Robert said: 'Yes.'

'Yes and no?' asked Jack.

'Aye. Yes and no,' said McLog. 'We saw a large object floating in the water, but on closer examination it turned out tae be Mrs McDoon out for a swim.'

Jack held up the twig again.

'This pollution . . .' he began.

'Is nothin' tae do with us,' said McLog again, very firmly. He looked at his watch. 'Right, your time's up, so if ye'd kindly leave . . .'

Jack stared at him in surprise.

'Leave? But . . .'

'Unless ye'd prefer Robert tae throw ye oot?'

All right, the time for friendliness is over thought Jack. Aloud he said, 'I warned you earlier, Mr McLog, that this article I'm writing . . .'

'Will never see the light of day,' said McLog smugly, and even Robert now had a sort of smug smile on his face. 'I checked with ma lawyers after ye went. If ye write anything suggesting that we're in any way doing anything wrong here, I'll sue for a million pounds damages. And I've already advised the papers so. No-one's going to touch your story. So good day, Mr Green.'

And with that McLog got up. Dorothy looked at Jack, shocked. Did this mean. . . ? She could tell by the look on Jack's face that it did indeed. McLog had won this round.

Jack and Dorothy got up, and as Jack did so his

glance suddenly caught sight of part of a small fishing boat covered with a tarpaulin in one corner of the room. Before McLog or Robert could stop him, Jack took a few strides, threw back the tarpaulin and revealed the boat, covered in the same eerie growths that had contaminated the twigs, with the name 'The Jenny' on its bow!

'Where did this boat come from?' Jack demanded.

'None of your business,' glowered McLog threateningly.

'On the contrary, it is very much my business. This boat belongs to my cousin Angus McIntosh, who disappeared four days ago.'

'Oh!' cried Dorothy shocked at the realization of what this meant.

McLog and Robert exchanged awkward looks, then McLog said in a low voice, 'We found it washed up on the shore of the loch and we brought it in for examination.'

'Was there any sign of Mr McIntosh?' insisted Jack.

'None,' said McLog gruffly. 'Now leave before Robert throws ye oot.'

'Shall I hit them, Jack?' asked Dorothy.

Jack shook his head.

'No,' he said. 'We'll go.' He turned back to the two men. 'But you haven't heard the last of this.'

Once they were safely outside the base, Jack and Dorothy stopped.

'Well, Jack, what do you think?' asked Dorothy.

'I think there's a chance that they may be holding my cousin Angus prisoner in there,' said Jack thoughtfully. 'So our next move is to work out how to get back in there tonight and find him.'

Chapter Eleven

Meanwhile, what of the monster that had run off after its encounter with M in his 'walking bush' disguise? The poor creature had been frightened out of its wits at seeing a bush coming towards it and terrified that it had bumped into a real monster of some sort. Because the monster was not a monster at all, but poor Angus McIntosh!

Four days earlier he had been out fishing on the loch when unfortunately his boat had capsized and he had had to swim to land. By the time he had pulled himself up on the shore, Angus had noticed that a change had started to come over him: eerie growths had begun to appear all over him, on his skin and his clothes, forming a covering that seemed like a mixture of fur and grass. Within a matter of minutes Angus resembled a large piece of vegetation.

His first thought was to run home, but then he stopped. He couldn't let his daughter Tammy see him like this, it would frighten her to death. Then he thought it over. He might frighten her at first, he decided, but as soon as she heard his voice and he told her what had happened it would be all right. That was when he discovered that he couldn't speak. The contamination had affected his voice.

Then he remembered that his English cousins would be arriving within the next day or so to stay for a fortnight's holiday with him. All right, his next thought was that he would leave them a written message. But when he looked down at his hands, the growths had knotted his fingers and thumbs together. It would be impossible for him to hold a pen!

From that moment life had become a nightmare for Angus McIntosh. He had kept hidden in the woods. He had managed to find a small stub of pencil and scrawled a note to Tammy warning her to stay away from the loch, but the pencil had broken before he could add more and tell her he was alive and all right.

At first he had tried to make it to a hospital, but when he had attempted to stop a car on the road to get a lift someone in the car had actually fired a shotgun at him! After that he had taken to lying low while he worked out what to do. He decided that he'd rather suffer this way while he waited for a chance to find a cure than be shot dead.

He had been hoping that his cousin Jack would help. Jack was an expert on environmental pollution, so he ought to know what this was and what to do about it. The problem, Angus decided, was getting to see him without frightening the rest of the family, particularly Tammy.

He had spotted Jack and the others arrive. As soon as he was able to he tried to get to Jack to tell him what had happened, perhaps in mime. Unfortunately when he nearly reached him, Jack had been grabbed by someone, and Angus had gone into hiding again, because at all costs Angus knew that he had to remain hidden. His encounter with that other monster, that walking bush, had terrified him. If there was a real monster on the loose then word would soon spread, and people would be out with shotguns hunting for it, and that would mean they would be hunting for *him*!

Angus came down the hillside, slipping slightly on the scree. Below him was a valley, and deep in the valley half-hidden behind some trees, he knew there was a cave. He hadn't been there for some time, but he hoped it was still accessible and hadn't been blocked by a rockfall, as sometimes happened.

It took him a full half-hour to get down to the floor of the valley, keeping under cover all the time, dodging behind rocks and bushes, but finally he made it.

Angus checked that no one was watching, and then hurried to the cave entrance. He was in luck, the entrance was still clear! He went in, deep inside the cave, determined to get as far out of sight as possible, until he was right at the very back of it. It was then that he felt a draught coming from the back of the cave. There was another cave further on, one he hadn't noticed before, and there seemed to be light coming from it.

Puzzled, and rather fearful, Angus pushed his way in through the narrow gap at the back of the cave, and then stopped in astonishment.

In front of him was another vast cave filled with all manner of scientific and electrical and electronic apparatus. It looked like an underground laboratory. At the far end of the cave was a pool of dark water.

On the rock floor at the centre of the laboratory was what looked like an operating table, and on it lay another monster like himself! Angus almost turned to run, then he stopped. The thing on the table wasn't moving.

He looked around the laboratory carefully. There seemed to be no sign of anyone. Maybe, the thought occurred to him, maybe there might be some stuff here that could cure him of this terrible condition.

Cautiously Angus crept down into the laboratory itself. Carefully he approached the figure lying unmoving

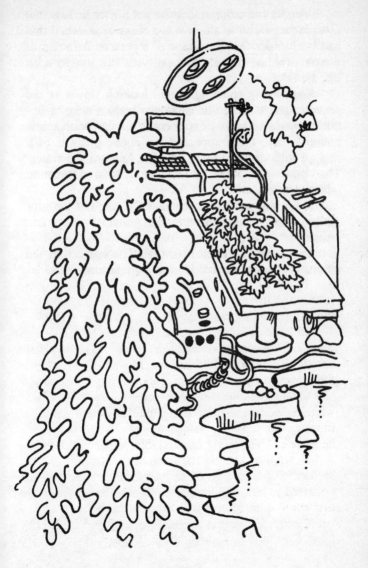

on the operating table, and as he got nearer he saw that it wasn't a person at all, it was a mass of seaweed that had been made into the shape of a person. Although it wasn't alive, he thought unhappily, it still looked a bit like he felt.

Angus was standing there, looking down at the seaweed shape, when he suddenly heard a deep throbbing sound, and the next second, in the pool a few metres away, there appeared the conning tower of a midget submarine pushing up from beneath the water. The pool obviously connected this underground laboratory to the loch!

There was a clang of metal as the hatch of the submarine was opened, and then the sound of voices and footsteps.

Angus stood frozen in shock. The owners of the laboratory had returned. He had only seconds to hide!

Chapter Twelve

The Vixen and Cuervo stepped down the short ladder from the submarine on to the rocky floor of the cave, Cuervo carrying a polythene bag containing another contaminated fish.

'I just hope for your sake that fish has got some good intestines,' snapped the Vixen, still irritated over what had happened.

'Is-a good fish!' insisted Cuervo. 'I know all-about fish, an is-a good fish!'

The Vixen took the polythene bag from him and emptied the fish into a jar.

'We may have got the fish intestines, but I'm still short of toad's brains,' she complained.

'Si,' said Cuervo, apologetically, 'is-a problem. Where we gonna get toad's brains? Their brains must be pretty small, hey?'

At this the Vixen stopped and looked at Cuervo's head. A toad's brains would be small, and so would an idiot's like Cuervo, she mused. I wonder. . . ?

'I believe we can improvise over the matter of the toad's brain,' smiled the Vixen. 'I think I have found one just as small.'

'Hey, great!' said Cuervo proudly. 'Is-a my being here help you, hey?'

'It certainly does,' said the Vixen with a smile, and she strolled over to the operating table and reached for a large heavy mallet. She was just about to pick it up, when she stopped. Something about the heap of seaweed on the table had changed. Then, as she looked at the monster, at its face, a shiver of excitement ran through her. The monster was looking back at her!

'Cuervo!' she yelled. 'Look at the monster! The electricity worked! Even without the toad's brains and the fish's intestine! It worked!'

'What?' said Cuervo.

Angus wasted no further time. He'd thought that he'd found a good hiding place lying on the mass of seaweed. He had been wrong.

He leapt off the operating table and made a run for the small entrance at the back of the cave.

'Hasta la vista!' croaked Cuervo, astonished at this sight.

'Catch it! Catch it!' urged the Vixen.

Cuervo needed no further urging, he rushed after the monster, but caught his foot in one of the electrical cables and tripped, falling headlong on the floor, giving Angus time to get through the small opening at the front of the cave.

'After it, you fool!' raged the Vixen. 'Don't let it get away!'

Then she and Cuervo scrambled up the rocks at the front of the cave, in hot pursuit of Angus.

* * *

Angus did what anyone does when being hunted, he made for home. Unfortunately for him, Cuervo and the Vixen were able to track him, following his heavy footprints and the pieces of the eerie growth that had fallen off him as he ran. So it was that as Angus reached his cottage, he was aware that his two pursuers were close behind him.

I mustn't put Tammy at risk from these people, he thought. Whoever they are, they look dangerous. Nor must I frighten her by suddenly rushing in.

For those reasons, instead of running into the cottage, Angus took refuge in one of his outside sheds, prepared to fight this weird man and woman, if necessary. He had just found a hiding place behind an old oil drum when the Vixen and Cuervo stumbled into the yard.

'We've lost it!' said Cuervo. 'It came up here, you can see by the tracks,' he went on, pointing at the marks on the muddy ground. He puffed out his chest, proudly. 'But the mud's so churned up round here, I can't see where to go now.'

'Well I'm not scrabbling around in this place much longer,' said the Vixen. 'These shoes are by Armani and I'm not going to ruin them in this mud.'

'But what we gonna do about the monster?' asked Cuervo. 'We got to get it back, si?'

The Vixen shook her head.

'We made that one, we can make another one. There's plenty more where that one came from, Generalissimo. And we've proved that we don't need toad's brains any more.'

There was the sudden sound of a car arriving, and the Vixen and Cuervo dived for cover. Luckily for Angus they chose a different part of the outbuilding from the spot where he was hiding.

A green car pulled up outside the cottage and the car door opened, and both the Vixen and Jose Cuervo nearly let out yells of shock and surprise as they saw Jack get out of the car.

85

'Caramba la hermesetas!' whispered Cuervo. 'You see who it is?'

'I do indeed,' whispered back the Vixen. 'Jack Green, my deadliest enemy!'

'*My* deadliest enemy!' objected Cuervo.

'He was my deadliest enemy before he was your deadliest enemy,' countered the Vixen.

Cuervo shook his head, refusing to accept it.

'No! Because of this man I go to prison where I have to wear a terrible suit that don't fit me properly!'

'He did me much more damage,' purred the Vixen. 'He defeated me in my previous greatest ever crime. And now he shall pay for it.'

Cuervo looked towards Jack, who had lifted the bonnet of the car and was checking something in the engine.

'He don't look like he's got that much money,' said Cuervo.

'With his life,' said the Vixen.

Jack had finished whatever he was doing with the engine, and he now closed the bonnet lid, wiped his hands, and strode towards the cottage.

'Come on,' said the Vixen. 'We've got some planning to do.'

And the two of them crept away, feeling a great glow of satisfaction that Fate had delivered their deadliest enemy into their hands for them to revenge themselves upon.

Jack's return to the cottage was greeted with some exasperation by Cynthia, who was surrounded by even more experimental equipment.

'There you are!' she said. 'I thought you'd gone off to Australia or somewhere! I think I've actually cracked

87

this antidote business but I've got nothing to test it on. Where are those twig samples?'

'Here,' said Jack, producing the bag from his pocket. 'But the reason I was later than anticipated is because I ran into some old friends of ours.'

'Oh?' asked Elizabeth, immediately worrying because from experience she knew that most of Jack's friends meant trouble of some sort or another.

'Dorothy Greckle and M from MI5.'

Everyone stared at Jack.

'What?'

Jack nodded.

'They confirmed what you said about the toxic waste contamination, Cynthia, and that in some way the McLog Marine Research Base is behind it.'

'I knew it!' said Cynthia triumphantly.

'What are we going to do about it?' asked Kate excitedly.

'We've already done one thing,' said Jack. 'Dorothy and I went to the base this afternoon to confront them with it.'

'And?'

'Unfortunately they denied everything and ordered us out,' said Jack unhappily.

'Well what did you expect them to do?' said Elizabeth haughtily.

'Did you find any sign of ma dad?' asked Tammy.

There was an awkward pause, then Jack said, 'We found his boat, "The Jenny". It's at the research base. According to Oscar McLog it had been washed up on the shore of the loch.'

There was a moment's shocked silence, then Tammy suddenly ran at Jack, punching him and kicking him, tears running down her face.

'Ye're lying!' she raged. 'Ye're lying!'

Jack managed to grab hold of her fists, and then he sat down, pulling her on to his lap.

'I'm sorry, Tammy,' he said, 'I wish I was, but it's the truth.'

Tammy stopped trying to hit him, and instead started to sniffle as Jack cuddled her closer.

'Though in my opinion it doesn't mean that your dad's been lost at sea,' added Jack. 'In fact I think they're lying at the research base.'

'What d'ye mean?' sobbed the upset Tammy.

'I think they might be keeping your dad at the base. They're certainly trying to hide something there! And if he's been contaminated in some way . . .'

Cynthia nodded.

'Jack's right. So when are we going in, Jack?'

Elizabeth looked first at Cynthia, then at Jack, a shocked expression on her face.

'Going in?'

'How did you guess, Cynthia?' asked Jack with a rueful smile.

'It's obvious, it's the sort of thing you'd do. Tonight, I suppose, under cover of darkness.'

'Right,' said Jack.

Elizabeth looked even more shocked.

'You mean you're actually intending to break in!'

'I discussed it with MI5 after they threw us out this afternoon,' nodded Jack. 'M says it will need five of us to carry out the search: two on watch and three searching. We have three already, me, Dorothy and M, so we need two more.'

'Me! Me!' yelled Kate and Michael.

'I want tae go! He's my father!' stormed Tammy.

'None of you children are going,' Jack said firmly.

89

'I don't want you in a position where you might get into trouble.'

'That's not fair!' protested Kate.

'For once your Uncle's Jack's right,' said Elizabeth. 'It doesn't happen often, but this time he is.'

'Well you can count me in, Jack,' said Cynthia.

'Thank you, Cynthia,' said Jack.

'I'll go as well,' said Edward.

Elizabeth gaped at her husband.

'Edward!'

'If Cousin Angus is in there, it's up to us to get him out,' said Edward.

'Hear, hear!' said Kate and Michael, supporting their father.

'No!' said Elizabeth firmly. 'Absolutely not! It could be dangerous, and I don't want Edward getting caught. We have to think of his position at the bank. Remember, Edward, Mr Snodgrass retires next year and you might be up for promotion. *I'll* go.'

This time it was Jack's turn to gape.

'You?'

'I can handle myself,' said Elizabeth indignantly. 'Don't forget, I was in the Girl Guides.'

'I think this is a little different from the Girl Guides, sis.'

'Listen,' snapped Elizabeth, 'I've had just about enough of you, Jack Green, telling everyone what they should and should not do. This is an important mission. You need someone you can rely on. I'm going. And that's that! Right?'

Chapter Thirteen

That night Michael and Kate sat with Tammy in her bedroom while they waited for Dorothy and M to arrive, and commiserated with each other about the injustice of not being allowed to go with the adults on the midnight raid on the McLog Research Base.

Tammy was particularly incensed. 'I don't see why I shouldnae go! He's my father after all! I hate them!'

'Why do you always hate people so much?' asked Michael, more than a little fed up with his sullen and nasty cousin.

'Because I do!' snapped back Tammy.

'You shouldn't hate them,' said Kate. 'Believe us, if he's in the base then Uncle Jack will find him.'

'Right,' agreed Michael. 'Uncle Jack may be a bit odd, but he's very good at solving things.'

'Aye, Uncle Jack's nae too bad,' admitted Tammy reluctantly. 'In fact I suppose he's all right, considering.'

'Considering what?' demanded Kate, leaping to the defence of her favourite uncle.

'Considering he's a grown-up.'

'Listen I've got an idea,' said Michael. 'We all want to go with them tonight, right?'

'Aye.'

'Yes.'

'So why don't we sneak out after they've gone and follow them?'

'That's a brilliant idea!' said Kate. 'They'll probably need our help, anyway. You know how useless adults are.'

'Aye,' agreed Tammy, but she couldn't help adding: 'That's the first intelligent idea ye've had since ye've been here.'

'Well if you weren't such a deadbrain maybe you'd have thought of it,' retorted Michael.

Before Tammy could snap back a rude answer, or throw something at Michael, Kate held up her hands to quieten both of them down.

'Stop it!' she said. 'If we're going to work together on this, then we've got to stop arguing. Otherwise the adults will find out what's going on. Right?'

Tammy and Michael glared at each other, then reluctantly both of them nodded in agreement.

'But how are we going to get there?' asked Michael. 'They'll be going in a car and we need to get there the same time they do!'

'There are two bikes in the shed,' said Tammy. 'Me and Kate can go on mine and you can use my dad's. And I know a short cut across the fields. That way we can leave after them but be there before they get there!'

A knocking at the front door downstairs made them all sit up.

'There they are!' said Michael, and the three children rushed for the stairs.

In the kitchen Jack was just opening the door to M and Dorothy as the three children arrived.

'Hello, Dorothy!' called Kate, glad to see her old friend again.

'Hello, you lot!' said Dorothy cheerfully, and she and Kate began swapping stories of what they had been up to since they had last seen each other.

Michael had to admit he was impressed. Both Dorothy and M looked very professional in their commando outfits and blackened faces.

'We're all ready, M,' said Jack. 'We're just waiting for Elizabeth. She's upstairs putting on her gear.'

'Right,' said M. 'Let's co-ordinate our watches.' He looked at his watch. 'I have 23 hundred hours.'

Edward checked his watch, and frowned. 'I make it two minutes to eleven.'

By now Cynthia had joined them and was examining her watch. 'And I make it one minute past,' she said.

M nodded. 'I make it one minute past *now*,' he said.

Cynthia shook her head. 'Now I make it *two* minutes past.'

'I make it one minute to,' said Edward.

'You make it one minute past as well?' asked M, double-checking and thinking that Edward had said 'one minute, too.'

Edward looked at him, beginning to feel bewildered.

'No, I make it one minute *to*.'

'That's what I said,' said M. 'You make it one minute past, too.'

'No, I make it one minute to, too,' said Edward.

Now it was M's turn to look bewildered. 'Too too?' he asked.

Jack, who had been listening to all this with an ever-broadening grin on his face, decided it was time he put his spoke in.

'Actually I make it three minutes past eleven now,' he said.

'And he makes it two minutes to,' said M.

'Who does?' asked Edward.

'You do.'

'No I don't.'

'Let's settle this,' suggested Jack quickly, worried that this procedure was going to go on until dawn. 'Dorothy, what time do you make it?'

Dorothy checked her watch. 'Five past eleven,' she said.

'That'll do,' said Jack, setting his watch. 'Everyone agreed on five past?'

Edward looked at his watch, disappointed.

'Now my watch has stopped,' he said.

At that moment the inner door opened and Elizabeth swept in, in full combat gear, complete with her face blackened with charcoal.

'Agh!' yelped M, momentarily alarmed before he realized who it was.

Jack grinned at his sister.

'My word, Elizabeth, you look stunning in that outfit. I don't think I've seen you look better.'

'Are we all ready?' asked Elizabeth, deciding to ignore her brother.

'All present and correct,' said Cynthia.

'Right, in that case you children had better get off to bed.'

'Absolutely,' said Michael sweetly. 'Goodnight, everyone.'

And the three children went out of the kitchen and up the stairs, Kate stopping to wish them a parting: 'The best of luck!'

Jack frowned as he watched the door shut after the three children.

'Well, that was nice and easy,' said Dorothy, pleased.

'A bit too easy, if you ask me,' said Jack suspiciously.

'If we are all ready, I suggest we go,' said M. 'Shall we check our watches again?'

The others shook their heads.

'Then let's be off!'

Jack, Elizabeth, Cynthia, Dorothy and M headed for the door, which Edward held open for them. At the door Edward stopped Elizabeth.

'Take good care of yourself,' he wished her.

'I will,' said Elizabeth, and gave Edward a big hug.

It was as Elizabeth stepped back that she realized most of the blacking had come off her face and was now all over Edward's, who looked like a chimney sweep after a hard day's work.

As the other four slipped out to the waiting car, M stopped to give some advice to Edward: 'A word of warning, Mr Stevens,' he whispered. 'We have reason to suspect that the people at the McLog Base are just the tip of an iceberg. There may be no depths to which they may not stoop to silence us. If you know what I mean.'

Edward gave a nervous gulp.

'You mean?'

M nodded.

'You, staying here all on your own, with no defences. You are a very brave man.'

And with that M slipped out after the others, leaving Edward feeling absolutely not very brave at all.

Upstairs, in Tammy's bedroom, the children had assembled. Michael had already made up a dummy in his bed and was helping the two girls make up dummies from pillows and blankets in theirs.

'Right,' he whispered when Kate and Tammy were

ready. 'Quietly out of the window. There's a drainpipe just next to it. I'll go first.'

And with that he climbed out of the open window, grabbed hold of the drainpipe, and began to climb carefully and quietly down to the ground.

Chapter Fourteen

At the McLog Base, McLog and Robert were sitting playing cards in a desperate attempt to stay awake. McLog had not been satisfied that their threat to sue Jack had 'finished him off', as he would have liked. As a result he and Robert had decided to keep an all-night watch at the base, 'just in case', but their vigil was taking its toll. Both men had been awake now for nearly forty-eight hours, and Robert could feel himself nodding.

'Do ye really think that Green man will come back tonight, Mr McLog?' he asked.

'He's bound to,' said McLog firmly. 'I feel it in ma bones. I know his sort. Always snooping around.'

There was a slight noise outside and Robert pricked up his ears.

'What was that?' he asked in a hushed whisper.

Both men sat stock still and listened, but there were no more noises.

'It's because we've been awake so long,' yawned McLog. 'We're starting tae hear things. We ought tae get some sleep.' He yawned again. 'I'll sleep first while ye take the watch. Wake me in an hour.'

'Right,' said Robert. He looked at his watch. It showed half past midnight. 'Shall I wake ye in a full hour, or *on* the hour . . . ?' he began, then the sound of snoring made him look up. McLog was fast asleep.

'All right fer some,' grumbled Robert. 'First watch, indeed.' He yawned. 'There are those of us who aren't so selfish as tae just fall asleep like that, leaving oor friends to face danger on their own. There are some of us who are determined tae stay awake, even though we havenae slept for nearly two days. There are some of us . . . ZZZZZ.'

And Robert's chin slumped down on his chest, and he snored, and slept.

Outside the base, M finished cutting through the security wire, and then, one by one, the team of five slipped under the cut wire and into the grounds of the McLog Research Base.

'Right,' said, M taking charge. 'Mrs Stevens and I will stay here on guard, while you three go into the base and search.'

'Right, sir,' said Dorothy, and she, Jack and Cynthia set off towards the actual building.

Elizabeth wasn't pleased. After all, she'd gone to a lot of trouble to put on all this gear.

'Why do we have to stay here while they go in there?' she demanded.

'In my case,' explained M, 'it is because I have some special glasses made for me by our man, P, that means I am able to see in the dark.'

And with that M put the glasses on, stepped forward, and smacked face-first into a tree, falling back with a cry of pain.

From their watching position in the undergrowth, Michael, Kate and Tammy groaned.

'Huh!' grumbled Michael. 'It's lucky we're here if that's the best they can do.'

'You stay here and keep watch while Kate and I go in,' whispered Tammy.

Michael was as put out as his mother had been at the idea of staying on guard while the others had all the fun.

'Me? But I want to . . .'

'We agreed we wouldnae argue,' said Tammy.

'And we are smaller so we can get in and out of small places easier,' pointed out Kate.

'Huh, I suppose so,' grumbled the reluctant Michael.

He settled down in the undergrowth to keep watch for any officials from the research base, and the adults from his own family team of 'commandos'.

When Kate and Tammy reached the building they discovered that Dorothy, using one of her many MI5 gadgets, had silenced the burglar alarm system, and had opened a small window, which was even now just ajar. Kate helped Tammy up through the window, and then Tammy pulled her cousin up, and the two girls slipped into the base itself.

Once inside, the two girls stopped, overawed at all the hi-tech equipment on display. In two chairs at a table, with playing cards scattered on the table, they could see two men fast asleep, snoring soundly. Just creeping past the two men were Uncle Jack, Dorothy and Cynthia.

Kate and Tammy crouched down and watched as Jack gestured for Dorothy and Cynthia to go one way, while he would go another. Kate indicated to Tammy to follow Dorothy and Cynthia, while she would go after Jack. Tammy nodded. As the three adults moved forward deeper into the base, in search of any signs of Angus, the two girls crept quietly after them. As they passed the tarpaulin-covered fishing boat, 'The Jenny', Tammy stopped, and a look of anger crossed her face. For a moment Kate thought her cousin was going to start kicking the two sleeping men, and she put her finger to her lips and shook her head at her fiery cousin. Tammy nodded, but with an angry scowl. Then Tammy headed after Dorothy and Cynthia. Kate waited till she was gone, then she followed Uncle Jack's trail.

Robert, meanwhile, gave a last snore, and then shook himself awake, just in time to see Kate's shoe vanishing round a corner as she disappeared after her uncle.

Robert's mouth dropped open. Intruders!

'Mr McLog! Mr McLog!' he whispered, and shook his boss, but McLog remained out cold. Robert hesitated. What should he do? Should he raise the alarm? But the last thing they wanted was for people to come investigating. Robert made a decision, he would track down these intruders himself and capture them. Then he and McLog would force them to tell him what they were after.

Jack, unaware of the fact that Kate was tailing him, crept down a corridor. What he was looking for was a room in which they might have Angus locked away.

He opened a door near him, but found it only contained machinery. He went on down the corridor, opening doors as he went, but found only rooms filled with stock, or more machinery, or equipment for testing water and marine plants.

Dorothy and Cynthia, for their part, were also not having much luck. All they had found so far were different tanks, some containing fish, but for the most part containing mud at different degrees of wetness.

Behind the two women, Tammy hid and watched them, becoming more and more disappointed as the search failed to show any signs of her missing father.

Kate crept forward in close pursuit of Jack, making sure that he never left her sight. Because she was concentrating so hard on watching her uncle she didn't notice that some distance behind her, Robert, in his turn was hiding and keeping and eye on her, determined to find out what she was up to.

After fifteen minutes of hard searching Jack turned a corner, and came face to face with Dorothy and Cynthia coming from the opposite direction. The unhappy expressions on their faces showed that they'd had as little success as Jack.

'Any sign of Angus?' Jack whispered.

The two women shook their heads, sadly.

'None, I'm afraid,' whispered Cynthia.

'It's all just mud and stuff,' added Dorothy.

Kate and Tammy had also joined up quietly, without the adults seeing and were standing in a dark-ened doorway a little way away. They were just filling each other in on details of their separate missions, when Tammy spotted Robert further back up the corridor, crouched next to a large tank of mud. Luckily for the two girls, Robert's attention was now totally on Jack, Dorothy and Cynthia as the three adults carried on their whispered conversation.

Kate followed Tammy's gaze, and saw that Robert was now creeping closer to Jack and the two women, obviously intent on catching them red-handed. Kate put her finger to her lips to warn her cousin not to make a noise, then she crouched low and hurried up a corridor, and then through a connecting room that she remem-bered from the search, with Tammy following closely behind her. This now placed the girls behind the unsuspecting Robert.

Closer and closer Robert crept to Jack, Cynthia and Dorothy, holding his hands ready to make a rush at them, when suddenly he felt two small hands grab his ankles. He looked down at his ankles in surprise, and the next second found himself being tipped into a large tank of slimy wet mud.

'Aaarghhhh!' spluttered Robert between mouthfuls of mud.

The three startled adults jumped and looked round, and spotted the floundering Robert but not the girls who had ducked down behind the tank. It was obvious that it would only be a matter of seconds before whoever was in the tank pulled himself out.

'I think it might be time for us to go,' suggested Cynthia, and with that she, Jack and Dorothy headed back up the corridor as fast as they could.

Kate and Tammy waited just long enough to give the three adults a thirty seconds start, then they, too, hurried off, intent on getting out of the research base and back to the safety of the cottage before they were discovered.

Robert struggled free from the tank of mud and stood for a moment, kicking his foot against the wall in frustration and watching great lumps of mud fall off on to the previously nice clean floor.

'Mr McLog!' he howled in anguish.

Chapter Fifteen

Meanwhile, back at the cottage, and mindful of M's parting words, Edward was still on the alert. In fact, he had been so much on the alert the whole evening that he was now nearly a nervous wreck. He had attempted to calm himself down by reading a good book, but the first one he picked out was called 'Murder in the Highlands', and that had put him off reading for the whole evening. Now, as he sat on a chair in the kitchen he listened for every noise, every creak, every possible footstep, waiting for these villains that M had warned him about to rush in suddenly, grab him and do terrible things to him.

Then all of a sudden he heard it! A definite footstep outside the door of the cottage.

Instantly Edward grabbed up the nearest heavy object, a large frying pan, and took his place beside the door, frying pan at the ready. The door opened as the intruder came in . . . and Edward struck! BONG!!!

'Argh!' gasped M, and fell to the floor like a stunned horse.

Then Elizabeth, Jack, Dorothy and Cynthia came in, and all stood gaping down in astonishment at the figure of M lying on the floor, slowly recovering.

'Edward! Really!' said Elizabeth

'I thought you were dangerous assassins,' said Edward apologetically.

'Well it's good to know that if we had been, Edward, you'd have been able to cope,' said Jack sympathetically.

'Are you all right, sir?' asked Dorothy, helping M to his feet.

'Fine,' said M groggily. He looked at Edward. 'I warned you we had to be on our guard. You never know when they will strike next.'

And then he staggered over to a chair and fell on to it, tenderly feeling his head for bumps.

'I'm going to check that the children are all right,' said Elizabeth, and headed for the stairs.

Luckily for the children they had all managed to get back up the drainpipe in time, and now they heard Elizabeth's footsteps coming up the stairs. Instantly Kate and Tammy jumped into their beds and pulled the duvets up around them, while Michael rolled under Kate's bed. Even as Michael disappeared from sight, the bedroom door opened and Elizabeth looked in. She saw what appeared to be two sleeping girls and gave a sigh of relief, and then pulled the door shut again and went back downstairs.

As soon as the door shut, Michael rolled out from under Kate's bed.

'That was close!' he said.

Then he and Kate became aware that Tammy was still lying covered up and was shaking slightly, obviously crying quietly to herself. Kate and Michael exchanged looks. Although their cousin had been horrible to both of them, they knew she must be feeling terrible about her father's disappearance, especially having seen his boat at the Research Base.

108

Tentatively, Kate got out of bed and padded over to Tammy.

'I'm sorry, Tammy,' she said. 'I hoped we'd find your dad there. I really did.'

Michael gave a heavy sigh. 'I'm afraid it looks like . . . he must have drowned,' he said sorrowfully.

Tammy sat up in bed, her face tear-stained, but still defiant.

'He's not drowned!' she said fiercely. 'He's still out there somewhere! I know it!'

Downstairs in the kitchen the adults were looking just as miserable as they discussed the same subject: Angus's disappearance.

'Well,' said Dorothy with a heavy sigh, 'Angus wasn't there.'

The others all sighed heavily as well.

'We'd better tell Tammy,' said Jack. 'It's only right that she should know.'

'I'll tell her in the morning,' said Elizabeth.

'If only, ' said Cynthia, 'we knew exactly what had happened to him.'

At that moment there was a loud thumping on the door. Everyone looked at each other in alarm.

'Who on earth can that be at this time of night?' said Dorothy.

'The police?' suggested Edward.

'I sincerely hope not, with us all dressed like this,' said Jack. 'We're going to have a hard time explaining it.'

The banging increased, a really insistent thumping at the door.

'We'd better answer it,' said Cynthia. 'Otherwise it'll wake the children.'

'Do we have any volunteers to open the door?' asked M, hesitantly.

'I will,' said Jack, and he strode to the door and opened it, and then everyone gasped in horror as, on to the floor of the kitchen fell the hideous figure of what appeared to be a hairy monster covered in growths.

Chapter Sixteen

There was a stunned silence as they all looked at the ghastly apparition lying on the floor, and then the figure started to move, holding out its hands appealingly, pointing at itself and at Jack, then pointing at photographs on the mantle above the fireplace.

Suddenly Jack realized what the creature was trying to say.

'Good Heavens! It's Angus!'

And, with grateful relief, the creature nodded, and then passed out on the floor.

The inner door opened, and Michael, Kate and Tammy rushed in.

'What's going on?' demanded Michael. 'We heard all this banging . . .'

His voice trailed off as they saw the figure on the floor. He gave a little shriek and leapt back.

'It's all right,' said Jack. 'He's alive, and the good news, Tammy, is that it's your father. He's come home.'

* * *

It was the next morning that all the explanations were made.

Cynthia had immediately returned to her laboratory equipment set up in the kitchen and had worked through the night, with Jack's help, to perfect the antidote to the

contamination, while Angus slept and slept, and Tammy watched over him. As the sun came up the weary Cynthia handed a small phial to Jack.

'There,' she said. 'I think that's it.'

'How will we know for sure?' asked Jack.

'There's only one way,' said Cynthia, 'and that's to try it on him.'

And so they woke the sleeping Angus, and then the whole family stood around in suspenseful silence and watched as Cynthia poured some of her antidote on to a spoon, and then poured it into Angus's mouth.

'From the experiment I carried out on one of the twigs,' said Cynthia, 'it took about three seconds to work.'

'One . . .' counted Michael.

And then, before their eyes, Angus began to change. It was as if all the hideous growths had suddenly turned to vapour and disappeared, and there, sitting in the chair was the old Angus they knew.

'Dad!' cried Tammy, and threw herself at him.

'Cynthia,' said Jack, 'you're a genius!'

'Really, Angus,' said Elizabeth, still feeling a bit peeved, 'you might have let us know. You've no idea how worried we've been.'

'I couldnae,' said Angus, his voice sounding croaky and strange, even to him. 'I was afraid tae come back here because I didnae want tae frighten Tammy. I thought I'd hide fer a day or two until my voice came back, but it didnae.'

'Why didn't you leave me a message?' demanded Tammy accusingly.

'With all these growths over ma hands I couldnae hold a pen. At first, anyway.'

'Then that note to Tammy saying "Don't go near the loch" . . . !' said Jack.

'Aye,' nodded Angus. 'That was from me.'

Jack turned to M, who had just watched the transformation of the hideous monster back into Angus with a sense of wonder.

'I think it's time we had some honesty in the picture and brought the whole thing out into the open,' he said grimly.

M gave a little shudder.

'Honesty? Are you aware of what you're saying?'

'Well we haven't got anywhere by all this sneaking around. We know that this stuff in the loch is causing these terrible mutations. The McLog Company must be taken to task for what they've done, and we've got to make sure this whole mess is cleared up now! We can't afford to have what happened to Angus happen to anyone else.'

'He's right, sir,' said Dorothy.

'Honesty. Truth,' mused M. 'It's an unusual concept, but in this case you might be right. Very well, Mr Green. We'll try it your way. What do you suggest?'

'We go back to the base and tell Mr McLog we know everything.'

* * *

While all this was going on, the Vixen was feeling more and more exasperated. She and Jose Cuervo had duplicated their experiment exactly: the mass of seaweed in human shape on the operating table, the contaminated fish, the electric currents, but nothing was happening. The mass of seaweed remained just that: a mess of inwert seaweed, with blue sparks jumping over it.

114

'Soon we have our monster again and then we can set it on the dreadful Jack Green, eh!' crowed Cuervo, looking forward to exacting his revenge on Jack with savage enthusiasm.

The Vixen switched off the generator with a sigh of deep annoyance.

'We could if this worked,' she snapped. She kicked the leg of the operating table in her anger, but the mass of seaweed just remained still and lifeless. 'I don't understand why the experiment isn't working now when it worked before.'

Cuervo watched her as she paced around the laboratory, thinking deeply.

'There's only one way to find out what we're doing differently and that's to get hold of the monster we made before, and dissect it,' she said at last.

'But it's gone,' said Cuervo. 'It ran away.'

'Then we have to find it, don't we, idiot! The question is: where is it?'

'So long as no one else has-a found it first,' pointed out Cuervo, and he gave a little shudder at the thought of the creature. 'I mean, you think of-a what it look like, hey?'

The Vixen turned to look at him, her mouth opening, and for an awful moment Cuervo thought she was going to attack him with something again, but instead she gave a laugh of delight and said: 'And I bet someone has, too! Oh well done, Generalissimo!'

Cuervo stared at her, baffled.

'What-a you mean?' he asked.

'It means that I bet we know where it is right at this moment.'

'We do? Where?'

'If you found a monster looking like that, where would you take it?'

Cuervo thought it over. This was like Mastermind. 'To the pictures?' he suggested.

'The police!' exclaimed the Vixen.

Automatically, Cuervo looked around in alarm, but the Vixen was continuing talking, expanding on her theme, 'And where would the police take a monster to? The research base by the side of the loch that says it's looking for a monster, of course!'

'Caramba, of course!' echoed Cuervo, suddenly realizing what the Vixen was getting at. He gave her a smug smile. 'I'm pretty clever to think of that all by myself, hey?' Then an awful thought occured to him. 'One moment, if they got it, how we gonna get it?'

'Simple. We will go to that research base and steal the monster and bring it back here.'

'Brilliant! I will go in-a there and tear that monster out with my bare hands!'

The Vixen shook her head.

'I think not. For once, Generalissimo, you will use intelligence instead of brute strength. We will recover our monster by cunning. We will go in in disguise.' And she gave a little smile. 'How do you feel about being a Drain Inspector?'

Chapter Seventeen

The visit to the McLog Research Base by Jack, Dorothy
and M wasn't as bad as Jack expected it to be, although
Robert was still fuming from his mud-bath at the hands
of the unknown intruders the night before. It started
with difficulty, of course, as the three walked in to
confront McLog and Robert, and were met with a very
curt instruction to leave the premises immediately or be
shot. M attempted to calm the situation down.

'If I might say a word . . .' he began.

'It's that bagpipe mender!' exploded Robert,
recognizing M, even without the kilt and sporran.

'Actually this is M, the Head of MI5,' said Jack.

M glared at Jack.

'That is supposed to be an official secret,' he
spluttered.

McLog and Robert exchanged shocked looks. MI5?
Then they were sunk! Twenty years in prison each!
Jack continued with the introductions, gesturing at
Dorothy.

'Agent 7 from the same organization. And I
am . . .'

'James Bond?' gulped Robert.

Jack smiled and continued, '. . . I am here to tell you
that we know all about the chemical contamination in the
loch and we have found an antidote to it.'

'There is nae contamination!' said Robert, desperate
not to incriminate himself.

'Shut up, Robert!' snapped McLog. He thought it over briefly. Just suppose, he thought, these people are telling the truth and they *have* found an antidote . . .? Aloud he asked: 'Ye're serious about this antidote?' adding quickly, 'if there *should* be any contamination . . .'

'We are deadly serious,' said Jack. 'My friend Professor Birdwood has made an antidote, and if we can make it in large enough quantities we can pour it into the loch and sort this problem out.'

McLog sat down heavily on a chair. For the first time in this nightmare there seemed to be some hope. He looked at Robert, then at the three visitors, and nodded.

'Verra well, Mr Green, and I must say what a relief it is that it's all oot in the open.'

Dorothy nudged M with her elbow.

'See, sir!' she whispered. 'Honesty and truth. It worked.'

M didn't seem very happy about this concept.

'You realize if this spreads, we spies could be out of work,' he commented.

'So, what's the next move?' asked McLog.

'The next move is for Professor Birdwood to come here so that you can work together,' said Jack. 'Have you got the facilities here for making the antidote up in large quantities?'

'Aye. It's what we've been trying tae do ever since this nightmare began, but so far with nae success.'

'What have you done up until now on making the antidote yourself?' asked M, knowing that there would be reports to write about this case.

'If ye'd like tae look around, we'll show ye,' offered McLog.

With that McLog led the way, with the three visitors and Robert following as he outlined the attempts of their experiments.

'What we've done so far is isolate the toxic cocktail and concentrate it so we can use it tae test possible antidotes. That's what's in all these pools of water, so make sure ye don't fall in. Over here . . .'

And McLog led the way to the mud samples, the sight of which made Robert shudder at the thought of being covered in the wet cold stuff the night before. Jack followed McLog, while M stopped and made a closer inspection of the pools containing the contaminated water, checking them for size, depth, all the sort of things that his bosses would like to see in the reports.

It was unfortunate for M that Dorothy had also decided to inspect the pools and was at that moment inspecting one just behind M. She stepped back to get a better view for her brooch-camera, and bumped into M.

'Aaaahhhhh!' cried M, and then there was a splash.

Everyone looked round, just in time to see M haul himself out of the water, soaked to the skin.

'Agent 7 . . .' he started to say, but he got no further. His voice packed up, and in front of their eyes M began to change as the eerie growths suddenly sprouted up all over him at an alarming rate, and within a few seconds M had gone and in his place stood the sort of monster that Angus had been.

'Oh Lord!' said the shocked Dorothy, 'I'm terribly sorry, sir!'

'He's hideous!' said Robert in an awed voice.

'But still dignified,' added Jack, seeing that this remark of Robert's had hurt M's feelings.

'Absolutely. Very dignified,' said Dorothy, hoping this would please her boss.

119

'But my heavens is he hideous!' said Robert again, and the other three nodded.

'I'll go and get Professor Birdwood and bring her back here with the antidote,' said Jack. 'I think it's best if we leave you here for the moment, M. We can't take you out in public looking like that.'

'I'm right with you, Jack,' said Dorothy, eager to get away from the look of extreme annoyance on her boss's face, which was obvious even under all the foliage. To M she added, 'We won't be long, sir. And I'm terribly sorry. No hard feelings, I hope.'

With that Dorothy put out her hand to shake M's, and found only what looked like a branch. Instead she settled for giving M a thumbs-up sign, and then she followed Jack out to the car.

Jack and Dorothy had only just driven off, when another car pulled up outside the Marine Research Base, and out stepped the Vixen and Jose Cuervo, both wearing white coats and carrying clipboards.

'Now remember,' said the Vixen. 'We've come about the pong from the drains.'

'Si,' nodded Cuervo. 'I got it.'

And with that the criminal pair went into the base.

When the bell rang in the base, McLog, Robert and the now monstrous M all jumped.

'That's possibly Green and the MI5 agent back again, having forgotten something,' said McLog.

'Say it isn't?' asked the nervous Robert, with one eye on M.

'Then get rid of them,' said McLog.

'Right,' said Robert, and he pushed through the double doors and into the reception area, where he came face to face with the Vixen and Cuervo.

'Yes?' asked Robert.

'Ah, good afternoon,' said the Vixen. 'We've come about the drains.'

Robert stared at her, mystified.

'The drains?'

'Si,' nodded Cuervo. 'The drains. Is-a how you say, the ping.'

'The pong,' corrected the Vixen.

'Si. The ping-pong.'

'I'm afraid we've had complaints from your neighbours,' the Vixen continued. She tapped her pocket. 'I have here a warrant to search these premises for blocked-up drains. I'm afraid I can't show it to you because it comes under the Official Secrets Act, but if you'd prefer me to bring the police in . . .'

'No no!' said Robert, still worried about the possible effects publicity about the toxic waste could have on the company.

'Good,' said the Vixen. 'In that case may we go in?'

And before Robert could stop her she had swept past him and through the double doors into the main room of the Research Base, Cuervo close on her heels.

McLog and the monstrous M turned as the doors opened, and looked in horror at their unexpected visitors. For their part, the Vixen and Cuervo looked at the monstrous M and exchanged secret smiles of delight. They had found their monster!

'I'm sorry, Mr McLog,' apologized Robert. 'They said it's about the drains.'

'I think I see the cause of the problem,' said the Vixen. 'It is obviously stuff from that large object that is blocking the drains up and causing them to smell. I'm afraid we'll have to confiscate it.'

McLog leapt in front of M as she stepped forward to grab the unfortunate Head of MI5.

'Wait! You cannot take him — this!'

'I'm afraid we can, and we must.'

'They threatened to call the police, Mr McLog!' blurted out Robert.

McLog's eyes narrowed with suspicion. There was something not right about this couple. The monstrous M nudged him, desperately. For his part, as Head of MI5 with a knowledge of most of the world's most dangerous criminals, M had recognized both the Vixen and Cuervo as two of the worst.

'Ye know, Robert,' said McLog thoughtfully, 'I think *we* ought tae call the police.'

Robert hesitated, then nodded. If Mr McLog said to call the police, then that was the thing to do. He was just reaching for the phone when suddenly:

'Oh no you don't!' snarled Cuervo, and from his pocket he pulled out a gun and blew the phone into smithereens. Immediately Robert stepped back and put his hands in the air.

'I'm sorry about that, but drain inspection is such a dangerous business,' purred the Vixen. 'If you'd tie these two up, I'll take care of our hairy friend.'

She grabbed M's arm in a painful hold and watched as Cuervo tied up McLog and Robert.

'There!' he said. 'All done! They're all tied up nice and tight.'

'Wonderful. Well, we'll be off.' She gave McLog and Robert one last smile that sent chills of fear through both of them. 'And any time you want anyone to look at your drains, don't hesitate to call on us. We do our best to satisfy.'

And with that the Vixen and Cuervo hauled the miserable and monstrous M out of the building.

Chapter Eighteen

When Jack and Dorothy arrived back at the cottage they found the whole family gathered around Cynthia as she checked Angus over, listening to his bare chest with a stethoscope, while Angus grumbled about it.

'It's not fair!' he complained. 'This sort of thing should be done in private. I feel like I'm on show in a circus!'

'All I'm doing is examining your chest and heart,' said Cynthia. 'Anyway, they're all worried about you.'

'And we've never seen a monster turn into a human being before,' said Michael tactlessly.

Before anyone could tell him off, the door opened and Jack and Dorothy rushed in.

'Cynthia!' said Jack. 'You're needed urgently down at the base with your antidote. I'm afraid M fell into a pool of contaminated water.'

The others gaped at him.

'You mean he's covered with that stuff like Angus was?' said Kate, doing her best to hide a grin at the thought.

'I'm afraid so,' said Dorothy.

'So now he really is an "undercover" agent,' said Michael, and burst into peals of laughter.

'I don't think that's in very good taste,' Jack ticked him off.

'Don't worry,' said Cynthia. 'I'll get my things and I'll be with you.'

'And this time we're coming with you,' said Kate firmly.

'Right,' agreed Michael, equally firmly. 'We want to see inside this base. Coming, Tammy?'

Tammy shook her head.

'I'm staying with ma dad,' she said.

'I think we should stay here as well, Edward,' said Elizabeth. 'If you ask me it's most undignified, everyone wanting to rush off to have a look at poor M just because he's turned into a monster.'

* * *

When Jack and the others arrived back at the McLog Base, they were startled to see that the doors were swinging open and that there was no sign of security of any sort.

'Something's happened,' said Jack grimly, and he rushed into the base proper, Dorothy, Cynthia, Kate and Michael following hot on his heels.

McLog, still tied firmly to Robert on the chairs, heard their footsteps and called out: 'Help! Help!' just as the door opened and Jack came in.

'Good Heavens!' said Jack, astonished.

'Quick! Get us out of this!' urged McLog.

As Jack and Dorothy worked to untie the two men, McLog told them what had happened: 'There were two of them. A man and a woman, both very suspicious. They said they'd come tae inspect the drains, but instead they tied us up and then they took M.'

'Did you recognize them?' asked Jack.

'I'd never seen them before. One was a woman, a really evil looking case. She had this superior sort of air aboot her.'

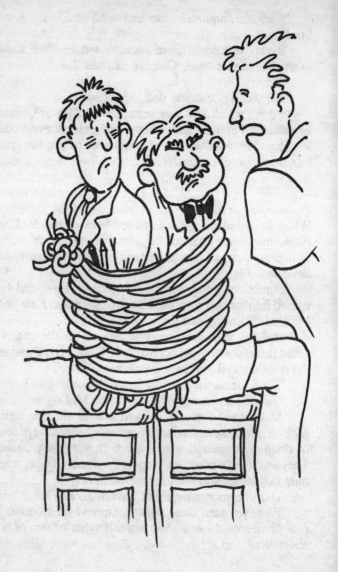

'The man sounded like he was Spanish or South American,' added Robert.

'A superior sort of woman, very evil, and a Spanish man?' pondered Jack. He shook his head. 'No, it couldn't be.'

'It couldn't be who?' asked McLog.

'The Vixen and Jose Cuervo,' said Jack.

'Ugh!' said Kate and Michael together, remembering their last encounter with that dangerous pair.

'No, not up here,' said Jack. 'The coincidence would be too great.'

'And what could the Vixen and Jose Cuervo possibly be doing up here in Scotland?' said Dorothy. 'It's not as if there's any terrible weapon up here they could get their hands on.'

'That toxic waste stuff is,' put in Cynthia. 'Just think what it did to Angus.'

'And to M,' added Jack.

'Exactly. If it was used as a weapon . . .'

McLog looked shocked at the thought.

'Heaven forbid! We never thought . . .'

'That's the trouble, people don't think,' said Cynthia. 'That's why this planet's in the mess it is.'

'What's our next move, Uncle Jack?' asked Kate.

'To get M back from this couple, whoever they are.'

'The trouble is, where could they be keeping him?' said Michael. 'They could be anywhere.'

'Wait a minute!' said Cynthia, a thought suddenly striking her. 'While I was examining him, Angus mentioned something about nearly being experimented on by a terrible pair, a man and a woman, in a laboratory in a cave not far from here. That could be them.'

'I bet it is!' exclaimed Jack. 'Right, Cynthia, you stay here and carry on working on producing the antidote with Mr McLog. Dorothy and I will go after M.'

'What about us?' asked Kate.

'We could do with some volunteers to help us if we're to produce this antidote in large enough quantities,' said Cynthia. 'Right, Mr McLog?'

'Call me Oscar. Aye, and ye're absolutely right. We're going tae need all the help we can get.'

'Good, that's settled then,' said Jack. 'You two stay here and help Cynthia. OK, Dorothy, let's get Angus and get him to take us to this cave.'

Chapter Nineteen

So it was that half an hour later, Jack and Dorothy were following Angus up a hillside towards the cave entrance that led to the Vixen's underground laboratory.

Elizabeth and Edward Stevens had been detailed to stay by the telephone 'just in case', though in case of what no one had actually specified. They had also been detailed to take charge of the reluctant Tammy, who had been set on going with her father, and would have, too, if Angus hadn't been very forceful in his instructions to her that he didn't want her going with him into what could be a dangerous situation.

Angus led Jack and Dorothy up the craggy hillside to the cave entrance, which was half-hidden behind a few small trees.

'This is it,' he said. 'We go tae the end and there's a small entrance which takes us intae the actual cave where the laboratory is.'

'I'm not sure if it's a good idea for you to come with us,' said Jack. 'After all, it hasn't been that long since you had a narrow escape from this pair.'

'That's why I'm coming with ye,' said Angus. 'You're going tae need all the help you can get.'

* * *

At that very moment inside the laboratory, the Vixen and Cuervo were tying up the unfortunate M. The

129

Vixen paused in the act of fixing the rope around M's wrists and looked at the monstrous figure.

'Do you know,' she said, 'it's strange, but the creature looks somehow familiar. As if I've seen it before.'

'Of course you seen it before, it's-a our monster!' said Cuervo.

'No, I meant before that. Does it remind you of anyone?'

Cuervo studied the shaggy figure. It looked to him like one of the bushes out on the hillside. He gave a laugh.

'George Bush?' he cackled. 'Get it? I make a joke! Bush . . .'

Obviously the Vixen didn't think it was very funny, because she didn't laugh, just carried on studying the shaggy figure thoughtfully. 'Do you remember the head of the British Secret Service? M? It just occurred to me that this thing reminded me of him.' She laughed. 'No no, it's just one of those things. Like when you look at a tree and think you can see a face.'

Cuervo laughed as well.

'Is-a good joke, hey,' he chuckled. 'The Head of MI5 looking like our-a monster!'

'I'm sure he'd be amused as well if he could hear us say it,' smiled the Vixen. 'Well, let's get on. Is the pool of toxic liquid ready?'

At the mention of the words 'toxic' and 'pool', M shuddered. Surely they weren't going to . . . to . . . to?

'Si, it's all ready.'

'Right, pop him in it and we'll see if he starts to mutate. If my calculations are correct he should grow another three metres and turn into a huge mass of that stuff.'

They *were* going to! Immediately M began to struggle, pulling against the ropes that tied him. There had to be a way to tell these people that he wasn't a lump of vegetation!

Cuervo tried to hold the struggling M still.

'Hey, see this?' he said. 'It's almost as if he understood-a you. You reckon we ought-a give it the anaesthetic before I throw it in?'

'Nonsense,' said the Vixen carelessly. 'It's just a plant. Gardeners do terrible things to them all the time. You don't see a rose making all this fuss when it's pruned, do you? Dump it in the pool.'

Cuervo nodded and was pushing the still struggling and monstrous figure of M towards the pool of bubbling toxic liquid, when suddenly Jack's voice echoed around the underground cave: 'Oh no you don't!'

Cuervo stopped pushing M, and he and the Vixen turned to see Jack, Dorothy and Angus stepping through the small opening at the front of the cave. The Vixen's face broke into a welcoming smile, like a cat greeting a mouse.

'Why Mr Green and friends! I wondered when you'd turn up. Nice of you to drop in.'

'Don't worry, sir! We're here now!' called Dorothy.

The Vixen and Cuervo looked at the mass of vegetation they had just been about to dump in the bubbling pool of toxic liquid.

'Sir?' said Cuervo, bewildered.

'So it *is* M after all!' crowed the Vixen with a deep-throated chuckle. 'How delightful! Thank you Dorothy! In that case I must insist you all come here, or he definitely goes into the toxic liquid.'

Jack looked at Angus.

'We'd better do as she says,' he said. 'Dorothy and

I have had dealings with this woman before, and she's likely to do it.'

Slowly Jack, Dorothy and Angus came towards Cuervo and the Vixen, the latter greeting them with a broad smile.

'Well well, Mr Green, how wonderful to see you again. Especially in circumstances like this.'

'I wish I could say the same,' said Jack, mentally kicking himself for being such an idiot as to rush into this without first consulting the police. Just because he had been worried about getting M back quickly, and now it looked as if they were all in trouble.

'Oh you will before I've finished with you, Mr Green,' said the Vixen. 'Tie them each to a chair, if you please, Generalissimo. Nice and tightly.'

'Is-a my pleasure,' smiled Cuervo and he set to work tying Jack, Dorothy and Angus each to a chair, while the Vixen paced around her prisoners.

'I have been planning some special revenge for you for a long, long time, Mr Green,' said the Vixen, almost chattily. 'By opposing me you hurt my feelings more than you can ever imagine.'

'The last thing I would ever want to do is hurt someone's feelings,' said Jack, ever polite.

'How touching. At first I was going to have you torn apart by wild animals.'

'A bit hard on the animals, don't you think, putting them to all that work,' commented Jack.

Cuervo stepped back from the prisoners.

'There!' he said. 'Finished!'

'Thank you, Generalissimo. But then, Mr Green, I thought . . . no, something simple is best.' And she

132

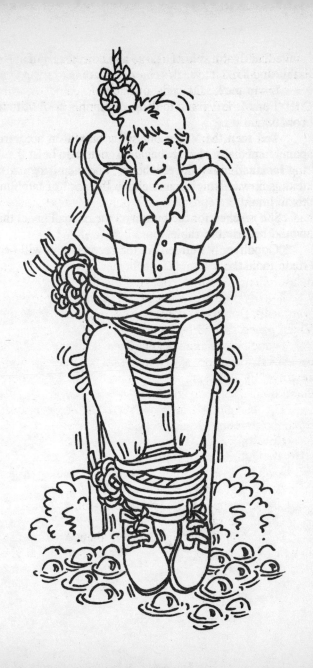

smiled, and took hold of a large hook on the end of a steel cable and fixed it to Jack's chair. 'I'm going to swap you.'

'Swap me?' said Jack, puzzled.

'For M. I'm going to drop you in this pool of toxic contamination.'

And then the Vixen pressed a button on a control panel, and the steel cable began to go up on a hoist, hauling Jack and his chair into the air, and then it swung so that Jack was hanging just above the pool of bubbling toxic liquid.

She reached for the button on the control panel that would release the cable.

'Goodbye, Mr Green. In ten seconds you will be a toxic monster.'

Chapter Twenty

Jack hung suspended in his chair, looking down in horror at the pool of bubbling toxic liquid beneath him. All right, *if* he got out of this then maybe Cynthia would be able to help him and M with her antidote, but this pool of hideous bubbling liquid looked worse than any of the toxic contamination he had seen so far.

Suddenly he remembered! Of course, Cynthia's antidote! He had a small bottle with some of Cynthia's antidote in his jacket pocket! If only he could reach it!

Although Jack's arms were tied to his sides, he could just move his fingers. Straining against the ropes that pinioned his arms to the chair, he managed to slip his hand into his jacket pocket and pull out the small glass bottle. Using his thumb he eased the top off . . . but then the bottle slipped from his hand and fell straight down into the bubbling pool.

'Goodbye, Mr Green! Hello, Toxic Monster!' smiled the Vixen, and she pressed the release button.

Instantly the cable dropped, and so did Jack and his chair, straight into the pool below him. Only now the pool had stopped bubbling; instead it just looked like a pool of ordinary water.

Jack hit the water with a splash and disappeared beneath the surface, and bobbed up again a few seconds later. He spat out a mouthful of water, and grinned at the horrified faces looking down at him: Dorothy, Angus and M (not that Jack could see M's face beneath the growths) looking at him, appalled because they expected him to change into some hideous monster; and the Vixen and Cuervo looking at Jack, appalled because he *hadn't* changed!

'What's-a gone wrong?' demanded Cuervo angrily. 'Why he no turn into a monster?'

'Because,' said Jack, spitting out more water, 'I managed to drop in an antidote that neutralizes the effects of the toxic waste. No more toxic monsters.'

The monstrous figure of M, delighted at hearing this, waited no more but jumped into the pool, almost landing on top of the unfortunate Jack.

The Vixen and Cuervo looked at one another, shocked. All their plans for world domination looked like vanishing!

Dorothy also took her chance. Getting to her feet she made a rush at Cuervo, the chair still tied to her hampering her movements enough to give Cuervo time to turn and face her, arms and legs ready in a stiff martial arts pose.

'Ha!' he said, defiantly.

Dorothy kicked him in the shin.

'Argh!' said Cuervo in an altogether different tone.

He pulled out his gun, which Dorothy, with one swift high kick, sent spinning from his hand into the pool.

'Owww!' he said, sucking his hurt fingers. 'Vixen!'

Then he noticed that the Vixen, instead of leaping to his defence, was heading for the midget submarine.

'Hey! Wait for me!' he called, and then he hurried after her.

Dorothy was just about to hobble after them, when she noticed that Jack had just bobbed up above the surface of the pool for the third time, still tied to the chair.

'Help!' said Jack, and spat out more water, and then he disappeared beneath the surface again.

* * *

The midget submarine dived down into the pool that led under the rocks and into the loch.

Inside the sub the Vixen fumed as she operated the controls.

'You fool!' she stormed at Cuervo.

'Me a fool?' defended Cuervo indignantly. 'What for?'

'Letting that woman kick that gun out of your hand! And now that cursed Jack Green has found an antidote.'

Cuervo's face took on a nostalgic look.

'I had an Auntie Dote once,' he said.

The Vixen looked at Cuervo, puzzled. This man had an antidote? For what?

'You did?' she asked.

'Si,' nodded Cuervo. 'Her real name was Auntie Dorothy but we called her Auntie Dote . . . .'

The Vixen suddenly realized what Cuervo was going on about.

'Not Auntie Dote!' she yelled at him. '*Anti*dote! What he's got gets rid of the toxic contamination!'

'My Auntie Dote used to get rid of everybody,' said Cuervo. 'She was some tough lady. One punch from her . . .'

The Vixen glared at him. She had had just about enough of this nincompoop and his reminiscences.

'Listen!' she snarled. 'I don't wish to hear about your wretched family any more! I am sick to death of your

137

family. We have to do two things. One, find out who's making this antidote and stop them. And two, get hold of some more contamination so that we can make our monster again.'

And as she operated the controls of the sub, she racked her brains: where would be the best place to get some more samples of the toxic contamination? And then the answer hit her! Of course! She remembered that when they had gone to the Marine Research Base she had seen, out of the corner of her eye, a boat half-covered with a tarpaulin, and the boat had been infested with those eerie growths! A sample from the boat would be all that she needed.

'That Marine Research Base!' she cried delightedly. 'Our cause is not lost!'

* * *

Back at the Vixen's cave, the soaking wet Jack and M (now restored to his normal self), and the dry Dorothy and Angus were just recovering, having got free of the ropes that had tied them up.

'We've got to alert the others!' said Jack urgently. He looked around the laboratory.

'What are you looking for?' asked M.

'With all this equipment there must be a phone here somewhere!' said Jack.

'Right!' said the others, and they all set to work searching among the hi-tech equipment of the laboratory for something that looked like a phone. Dorothy was the one who found it first.

'Got it!' she cried delightedly, and she began to pick out 999 on the dialling buttons.

Simultaneously, a buzzing sound made Jack look

round, and he spotted a small mobile telephone just by his hand. Perhaps it was the police, or Edward or Elizabeth, who had somehow found out this number! Urgently he snatched it up.

'Hello?' he said.

Whatever the person at the other end of the line said, Jack couldn't hear, all he could hear was Dorothy behind him bellow loudly, 'Hello, this is an emergency!'

Jack turned to Dorothy, the phone still held to his ear.

'Can you keep your voice down! I can't hear,' he said.

Dorothy, for her part, heard the man at the other end of the line ask her to keep her voice down because he couldn't hear, and she frowned. How odd! she thought. But she dropped her voice to a whisper and croaked almost inaudibly, 'Hello?'

Jack listened to the woman at the other end of the line speaking in a whisper so low he could hardly hear her, and frowned in irritation.

'Can you speak up, I can't hear you!' he said.

Dorothy heard the man at the other end of the line ask her to speak up and gave a snort of annoyance.

'I wish you'd make your mind up!' she snapped into the phone. 'First you want me to keep my voice down, then you want me to speak up . . .'

As he heard Dorothy say all this, Jack realized what had happened, and he turned to Dorothy, who was still on the phone.

'Who am I speaking to?' demanded Dorothy.

Jack put his phone down. 'You were speaking to me,' he said. 'These are internal phones.'

Dorothy looked at the phone in her hand for a second, baffled. Then the penny dropped and she replaced the phone.

'Gosh!' she said. 'Weren't we a couple of idiots!'

But Jack was already heading for the small entrance at the back of the cave.

'We'll have to get back to the cottage and use the phone there,' he said. 'Come on!'

* * *

At the cottage the telephone was the centre of attention for Elizabeth, Edward and Tammy, who all sat waiting for it to ring.

'I wish Kate or Michael would phone to say that they're all right,' said Elizabeth.

'I wish Jack would phone to say everything's all right,' said Edward.

'I wish my dad would phone to say he is all right,' said Tammy.

Then the phone rang, and they all jumped. Elizabeth was the first to grab it up.

'Yes?' she gasped.

'Hello,' said the voice at the other end. 'We are a firm called Wonderful Windows and we are doing a special promotion in your area for a new sort of double-glazing . . .'

'No thank you,' said Elizabeth shortly, and she slammed the phone down.

As Edward and Tammy watched her, she got her coat and began to put it on.

'Where are you off to?' asked Edward.

'I'm not waiting here any longer,' said Elizabeth. 'I'm going to the base to see how Kate and Michael are.'

'But Jack said . . .' began Edward.

'I don't care what Jack said. They are my children and I'm worried about them.'

And with that she swept out of the house. Edward and Tammy watched her go, and watched the door still vibrating after she had slammed it shut behind her.

'I'm worried about my dad,' said Tammy.

Edward sighed.

'I'm just worried,' he said.

* * *

At the McLog Research Base, Kate and Michael had been working with Cynthia Birdwood, Oscar McLog and Robert, and now they had a stack of huge drums filled with the antidote, all connected to a pipe that in turn joined to a valve that led directly under the ground and into Loch Noch itself.

'There!' said Cynthia proudly. 'The antidote, all ready to pump into the loch. All I have to do is open this valve . . .'

And she took hold of the valve and was just about to turn it, when the door crashed open and there framed in the doorway, both holding guns, were the Vixen and Jose Cuervo.

'Oh no you don't!' said the Vixen.

Cynthia and the others looked at the pair, shocked.

'Come on! Hands up!' snarled Cuervo.

Slowly Cynthia, Kate, Michael, McLog and Robert put their hands up. The Vixen smiled.

'So! The famous Professor Cynthia Birdwood! I should have known that if anyone could come up with an antidote to this toxic contamination it would be you.' Turning to Cuervo, she said, 'Tie them up.'

Cuervo nodded. He was getting quite used to tying people up lately. Maybe, he thought, there was an award for the Best Knots that he could win.

While Cuervo tied the five up, the Vixen paced around the base searching for the boat she had glimpsed before. She found it, just hidden out of sight behind the stack of drums. She slipped on a pair of gloves and began picking off pieces of the eerie growth and placing them in a plastic bag. Cynthia watched the Vixen as she did this, and shook her head sadly.

'I can't understand why someone with a brain like yours should devote her time to destroying things, Vixen,' said Cynthia. 'Science can be used for good as well as for evil. With your intelligence you could help make this world a wonderful place.'

'Yes, I can't understand that, either,' smiled the Vixen. 'Interesting, isn't it? But then, I *am* interesting.'

'OK. All done,' said Cuervo, standing back and admiring the wonderful knots he had tied. Yes, certainly, he would enter for the Nobel Prize for Knots at the next Olympics, or whenever it was held.

'Good,' said the Vixen, putting the plastic bag with the growths safely away. 'Then we can go.'

Robert heaved a sigh of relief.

'You mean you're not going to shoot us?' he said.

Michael glared at Robert, annoyed.

'Do you have to give people ideas?' he said.

The Vixen smiled.

'Of course we're not going to shoot you,' she said.

At her words the five prisoners relaxed, but then stiffened again as they saw her take what looked ominously like a bomb from her bag: five sticks of explosive with a large old-fashioned clock attached to them by wires.

'We're going to blow you and this place up,' she smiled, and she fixed the bomb to the valve that controlled the flow of the antidote.

They stared at her in horror.

'Blow us up?' croaked McLog, shocked.

'It's very efficient,' explained the Vixen. 'It will destroy the antidote, and also stop you making any more, Professor.'

'Is that necessary?' asked Cynthia. 'You could at least let the children go.'

'And the adults!' Robert added hopefully.

The Vixen shook her head.

'And leave witnesses? I'm afraid not. Come, Señor Cuervo.'

With that the pair headed for the door, which opened as they approached and Elizabeth entered in a hurry, in search of Kate and Michael. She walked straight into the Vixen.

'Aaargh!' said Elizabeth, recognizing the evil pair.

Before Elizabeth could make a run for it, the Vixen had grabbed her with one hand and thrust the barrel of a gun into her neck with the other.

Cuervo gestured towards the five tied-up prisoners

'Shall I tie her up as well?' he asked, keen to continue with his knot-tying practice.

'We haven't got time for that,' said the Vixen, pointing towards the ticking bomb. 'We'll take her with us as a hostage.' She turned towards the five tied-up prisoners and gave them a big smile.

'I do hope you enjoy your last few moments,' she said. 'I can assure you that, for you, today is going to go with a bang!'

And then the Vixen pushed Elizabeth through the double doors and out of the base, Cuervo following.

Kate, Michael, Cynthia, McLog and Robert looked at one another, then at the ticking bomb as the clock on it continued its remorseless countdown, and each of them shuddered in horror.

Chapter Twenty-One

Edward and Tammy were still waiting by the phone when the door opened and Jack, Dorothy, Angus and M entered.

'Dad!' cried Tammy, and she rushed to cuddle Angus, while Jack asked Edward, 'Where's Elizabeth?'

'She went down to the base to see how Kate and Michael were.'

A bolt of fear went through Jack. It had occurred to him that the Vixen and Cuervo could well be heading for the McLog Base. He rushed to the phone, picked it up and dialled the base. At the other end of the line he could hear the phone ringing and ringing. He slammed the receiver down.

'There's no answer from the base.'

'That's odd!' said Dorothy.

'More than odd, it's downright worrying.' Jack turned to M. 'M, you'd better get on to the emergency services.'

'Straight away,' said M.

He picked up the phone as Jack turned to the others.

'I'm going to the base!' Jack announced.

'Count me in!' declared Dorothy.

Then they all stopped and turned to M, as they heard M say into the phone, 'Is that Harrods . . . ?'

M looked up from the phone at their accusing stares.

'They're always the first people I phone in any

emergency,' he said defensively. 'You never know when you're going to run out of supplies.' He sighed. 'But very well, if you insist on my contacting the *other* emergency services . . .' And he pressed down the connection, and then started dialling 999.

Edward was putting on his coat.

'I'm coming, too!' he said. 'If Elizabeth's in trouble then my place is by her side!'

'I'm coming as well!' said Tammy, determined to get in on all this activity.

'Oh no you're not!' said Angus firmly. 'After seeing what the people we're dealing with are capable of, you're staying here with me.' He turned to Jack, Dorothy and Edward who were even now rushing out of the door. 'Phone us if you need help, Jack!'

* * *

Inside the midget submarine Cuervo was practising his knot-tying on Elizabeth, while the Vixen steered the sub back towards the underground cave.

'If I ever get out of this . . .!' stormed Elizabeth furiously, while Cuervo frowned at the two pieces of rope in his hands. Was it right over left or left over right?

'You won't,' said the Vixen confidently.

'Don't you be too sure!' said Elizabeth challengingly. 'I shall hunt you down wherever you hide. No mountain will be too high, no valley too deep . . .'

'No mouth too big,' groaned the Vixen. 'Do tell her to keep quiet, Señor Cuervo.'

'Keep quiet, or else!' snarled Cuervo menacingly.

'Or else, what?' said Elizabeth defiantly.

Cuervo thought it over. Or else, what? Then he gave a superior sneer.

147

'Or else *I* keep quiet!' he smirked, and thought proudly: Ha! That told her!

* * *

At the McLog Research Base, Cynthia had been desperately struggling to reach the ticking bomb, but it was just out of her reach. She fell back on to the nearby bench, her whole body aching with the effort of stretching against the ropes that held her to the wall.

'It's no good!' she said.

They all looked at the clock as the countdown ticked on. Only forty seconds to go!

Suddenly the door crashed open and Jack rushed in, Dorothy and Edward close behind him.

'Watch out!' yelled Kate. 'There's a bomb there!'

Immediately Dorothy stepped forward, flexing her fingers.

'Leave this to me,' she said determinedly. 'I'm trained in bomb disposal technique. When I was at Special Agent Training School . . .'

'It's going to go off in ten seconds!' McLog screamed impatiently at her.

'Right!' said Dorothy, and she strode over to the bomb and examined it. Two wires connected the explosives to the clock detonator, one brown wire and one blue.

'Eight seconds to go. . .!' gulped Michael.

'I have to disconnect one of these two wires,' explained Dorothy. 'The trouble is, if I pull the wrong one out, the bomb will blow up.'

'Please decide quickly, Dorothy,' gulped Jack, starting to sweat. 'There are only three seconds left!'

Dorothy frowned at the wires. Which one was it, blue or brown. . . ?

'Two seconds!' said Michael hoarsely.

'One. . .!' shrieked Kate.

Oh well, thought Dorothy. It's a fifty-fifty chance. And she pulled out the blue wire.

There was a terrifying pause, then everyone heaved a sigh of relief, this collective sigh turning to a collective hiccup as the alarm on the old-fashioned clock went off.

'What I was going to say,' said Dorothy, 'was that at Special Agent School I always used to pull the wrong wire.'

Jack and Edward were in the meantime untying the five prisoners.

'Where's your mum?' Edward asked Kate and Michael.

'The Vixen and Jose Cuervo took her as a hostage,' said Kate.

'What!' said Jack and Edward together.

'They also took some of that stuff from Angus's boat,' said Michael.

'The Vixen obviously plans to use it to grow some more toxic contamination,' explained Cynthia, rubbing her arms from where the ropes had cut into her skin. 'If you want my opinion the Vixen will need her laboratory equipment to synthesize the sample. My guess is they've gone back to her cave.'

'Then that's where I'm going!' said Jack.

'So am I,' said Edward. 'I'm going to get Elizabeth back!'

'We're coming as well!' declared Michael.

'No you're not,' said Jack.

'She's our mother!' Kate protested.

'And the Vixen's very dangerous,' Jack reminded them. 'If you want to help then phone M at the cottage and tell him what's happened.' He turned to Edward and Dorothy. 'To the cave!'

Chapter Twenty-Two

Angus and Tammy watched as M listened to whoever was speaking at the other end of the telephone.

'You don't say!' said M, obviously shocked. He shook his head as even more tragic news came over the phone. 'You don't say!'

Angus and Tammy exchanged worried looks. This was obviously terrible news. M looked even more horrified.

'You don't say!' he said for the third time. Then he put down the phone, shaking his head in horror.

'Who was it?' asked Angus.

'He didn't say,' said M, 'but it sounded like Michael. The Vixen and Jose Cuervo have kidnapped Elizabeth. Jack, Edward and Dorothy have gone to the cave after them.'

Angus's face darkened.

'They're vicious people!' he said angrily.

M glared at him.

'How dare you!' he said. 'Agent 7 is a most gentle soul.'

'I'm talking about the Vixen and Jose Cuervo,' said Angus.

'Oh,' said M, embarrassed.

'If they're in trouble we must help them!' declared Angus fervently.

M frowned at him, puzzled.

'Help the Vixen and Jose Cuervo?' he asked.

'No! Jack and the others.' And Angus headed for the door, Tammy following him.

M shook his head before going after them.

'I wish people would say what they mean,' he complained.

* * *

At the Vixen's underground laboratory she and Cuervo were just putting the finishing touches to their escape plan. They already had the equipment the Vixen needed stored safely on board the submarine, now she was packing the eerie growths from Angus's boat into a shoe box, while Cuervo made up another bomb, a much bigger one this time. This bomb would destroy the underground cave and any evidence that the Vixen and Cuervo had ever been there.

Near to the edge of the underground pool Elizabeth had been tied securely to a post. Next to her was a large glass box, its lid lying next to it.

'This is a good bomb!' said Cuervo proudly. 'This one will blow this whole place sky-high. There will be nothing left!'

'Jack will get here before it goes off! You'll see!' said Elizabeth defiantly.

In fact she didn't feel as confident as she sounded, but she didn't want this pair of evil criminals to know that.

The Vixen put the box of growths down on the table and smiled at Elizabeth, and her smile sent shivers of fear up Elizabeth's back.

'You know, it's just possible he will,' she said. 'With Mr Green, anything is possible. That's why I'm going to arrange a surprise for him.'

And the Vixen picked up one of two other boxes that were on the table.

'The bomb is now all set and ticking!' said Cuervo proudly.

'Right,' said the Vixen. 'Pop it in that glass box. Then take the box with the growths for our new toxic monster to the submarine.'

'Hey! We're still gonna take over the world, hey!' cried Cuervo delightedly, and put the ticking bomb into the glass box by Elizabeth, just out of her reach. Then he picked up one of the two boxes from the table and set off for the submarine. If the Vixen had been looking she would have noticed that, unfortunately for them both, Cuervo had picked up the wrong box, *not* the one that the Vixen had so carefully put the eerie growths in. But the Vixen hadn't been looking because she was approaching the glass box with the bomb ticking away in it.

'My first surprise,' said the Vixen, 'one of my little pets to guard the bomb.'

And the Vixen shook the box into the glass case, and out fell a large and hairy tarantula. The sight of the spider as it crawled over the bomb sent shivers up Elizabeth's spine. Before the spider could crawl up the glass, the Vixen pushed the lid into place.

'There!' said the Vixen triumphantly. 'My furry little friend will look after the bomb. And now some more puzzles for your interfering brother.'

And the Vixen went to one of the control panels and started to press various switches. Elizabeth watched her in mounting horror. What terrible torture was the Vixen planning?

'You'll never make me talk!' said Elizabeth bravely.

'The problem is getting you to shut up,' commented the Vixen acidly.

'Whatever you're going to do to me. . . !

'I would have thought that was obvious,' said the Vixen. 'I'm going to blow you up, along with all the evidence. And just in case anyone comes along to try and save you, I'm setting a series of alarms that work on invisible infra-red beams. If anyone breaks one of the beams, then a trap is sprung, a very simple sort of trap. The whole of this floor had a series of steel nets all over it. When the trap is sprung, the net goes up, taking with it whoever has sprung the trap. A mixture of hi-tech and low-tech. Very simple, but very effective.' The Vixen pressed a final switch, and then went over to Elizabeth.

'And so that you don't warn him . . .'

Elizabeth shrank back from the Vixen as she produced a strip of sticking plaster and stuck it painfully across Elizabeth's mouth.

'There,' she said, satisfied. 'I think that will shut you up.' She looked at the ticking bomb in the glass box, with the tarantula crawling over it. 'I see by the clock you have fifteen minutes left. Just think what you can do in fifteen minutes.' And she gave Elizabeth a smile. 'You can worry a lot. Goodbye.'

* * *

At the McLog Research Base, Kate and Michael watched as Cynthia, McLog and Robert monitored the antidote as it was pumped into the loch.

'I reckon we've done as much as we can here,' Michael whispered to his sister. 'The antidote's on its way into the loch, so our job's done. I think we ought to help Dad and Uncle Jack rescue Mum.'

'That's just what I was thinking,' agreed Kate.

156

And the two children slipped out of the room, unnoticed by the three adults.

'How long will it take for the antidote tae take effect?' McLog asked Cynthia.

Cynthia thought the problem over. 'Well, it's a big stretch of water . . .' Quickly she did some mental calculations. 'Forty kilometres by fifteen by . . . in cubic metres . . . plus the saline factor . . . What's the tide position?'

'Outgoing as of an hour ago.'

'Then I'd say in about four hours the loch should be clear. Let's check the pump pressure again.'

A sudden 'bleeping' sound from the radar screen drew the adults attention.

'What's that?' asked Robert, surprised.

As they watched they could see five large 'blips' appear on the screen, moving across it like a shoal of fish. But these were no fish. By the size of the blips they made, these were enormous.

'Increase the volume on the sonar,' said Cynthia.

McLog turned up the volume on the sonar, and as the three listened the room was filled with noises from underwater, noises like cows mooing crossed with the sound of whales singing. The three looked at each other in awe. Robert was the first to break their silence.

'They're living creatures! Enormous living creatures!'

'Maybe they're whales?' suggested McLog. 'There's nothing else I can think of that size.'

Cynthia shook her head. 'That's not whale song.'

'Ye don't think . . .?' said McLog, his voice hushed with awe at what he was thinking.

'I do,' nodded Cynthia. 'Huge creatures of that size. They can only be what is commonly termed the Loch

Noch monster. In this case a whole family of them. What we have here is a shoal of dinosaurs previously thought to have been extinct, a family of plesiosaurii!'

'And they're heading straight towards the point where the contamination is at its worst!' pointed out Robert. 'We'll never get the antidote intae that part of the loch in time! They'll be contaminated!'

Chapter Twenty-Three

In the underground cave, Elizabeth watched the clock on the bomb as it ticked off the seconds. Behind her she heard the sound of the midget submarine as it submerged under the water with a hiss of bubbles and the throb of its engines.

I hope that Kate and Michael were saved from the bomb, she thought. If Jack could have saved them, then she knew that he would have. Oh, if only Jack were here! And then she realized that even if he were there was little he could do with the cave booby-trapped as it was.

'It's all right Elizabeth! We're here!'

She looked round as the voice called to her. It was Edward! And with him were Jack and that MI5 agent, Dorothy!

'There's a bomb!' said Jack, pointing at the explosives and the clock ticking away in the glass box near to Elizabeth. 'The Vixen and Jose Cuervo are certainly leaving them lying around.'

'Don't worry,' said Dorothy confidently. 'I know which wire to pull out now. It's the blue one. Or is it the brown one?'

And with great assurance she began to stride across the floor of the cave towards the bomb, Jack and Edward close on her heels, all three of them heading towards one of the invisible infra-red beams. Frantically Elizabeth shook her head and made gurgling sounds to stop them.

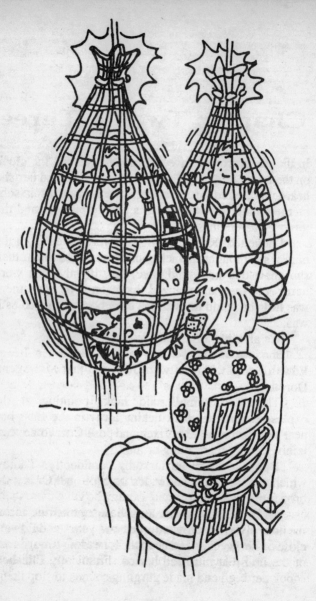

'What's the matter?' asked Jack, puzzled by Elizabeth's actions.

Suddenly Dorothy spotted the spider.

'Argh!' yelled Dorothy. 'She's trying to tell us there's a tarantula in that box with the bomb.'

'In that case we'll just get Elizabeth out of here,' said Jack. And he gave a grin as he stepped forward. 'Don't worry, Elizabeth, in a few seconds we'll be . . .'

Then the three of them walked straight into an infrared beam. The next second two huge nets made of steel wire came up from the floor and sailed up towards the ceiling, one of them taking Jack, the other snatching up Dorothy and Edward.

Jack, Dorothy and Edward clung inside the nets, trapped, and gaped down at Elizabeth and the ticking bomb in astonishment.

'In a few seconds we'll be what?' asked Edward, still stunned.

'Hanging from the ceiling in a net,' said Jack, feeling like a complete idiot.

'It's all right! We're here!' called M's voice, and they looked towards the back of the cave and saw M, Angus and Tammy struggling through a small hole.

'Be careful, M!' called Jack. 'There's a bomb over there and there are also booby traps like this one that caught us.'

M gave a superior smirk.

'Don't worry, I am an expert on booby traps,' he told them. Turning to Angus and Tammy he gave them their instructions: 'The secret is to keep close together and make sure you always look where you put your feet.'

And with that M stepped forward, Angus and Tammy following his instructions and sticking to him as if they were glued.

'We'll have you out of there in a jiffy, Mrs Stevens!' M called, and stepped straight into another of the infra-red beams.

There was the flash of a net hurtling up from the floor, and the next second M, Angus and Tammy were also dangling helplessly from the ceiling in a huge steel net.

'That's a very well kept secret, M,' commented Jack acidly.

All eyes turned to the bomb, which now showed only two mintues left before it exploded.

* * *

Inside the submarine, the Vixen checked her watch.

'The bomb should be going off any moment now,' she said with gleeful delight.

'And then all the witnesses against us will be gone, and we will be able to make the new monster!' chortled Cuervo.

He picked up the shoe box he had brought on board the submarine and kissed it.

'Hooray for "instant monsters"! ' he crowed, and he opened the box and turned it upside down on the control panel. Then he and the Vixen stared at the control panel in horror. This wasn't a boxfull of eerie growths from Angus's boat, this was . . . a very large and very hairy tarantula!

'Aaarghhh!' yelled the Vixen and Cuervo in unison.

* * *

The bound and gagged Elizabeth and the others dangling

162

from the ceiling in the two nets watched helplessly as the clock on the bomb ticked away the seconds. One minute five seconds to go.

'I say, sir . . .?' called out Dorothy.

'What is it, Agent 7?' asked M.

'I wonder if you had any useful gadgets on you for getting out of metal nets? You know: P?'

At this, Tammy's face expressed her disgust.

'Pee?' she said. 'Yurk!'

'I'm talking about Agent P,' said Dorothy stiffly. 'He supplies all our secret equipment. Things for getting out of steel nets, that sort of thing.'

' "P" is supposed to be a secret, Agent 7,' M rebuked her.

'Oh,' said Dorothy, shamefaced, realizing she had betrayed yet another Official Secret.

'O?' said Angus, puzzled. 'I thought you said his name was "P".'

'I didn't mean "O" as in "P", I meant "O" as in "Oh",' explained Dorothy. 'He used to be called "Q".'

Suddenly there was a shout of delight from Edward who had seen Jack drop to the floor, having struggled free from his net.

'I'm out!' Jack yelled.

'How did you do that?' demanded M, rather put out that once again this amateur should steal a march on the professionals.

Jack smiled. 'Paul Daniels showed me. Only he does it quicker.'

A sudden call of 'Uncle Jack!' from the back of the cave made everyone look round, in time to see Michael and Kate scrambling down the rocks.

'Get out, the pair of you!' yelled Jack. 'There's a bomb about to go off!'

Kate and Michael stopped, not rushing forward, but not retreating either.

Jack hurried to the glass box that contained the ticking bomb and the tarantula.

'Be careful of that spider, Jack!' called Angus. 'It looks like a tarantula tae me!'

'Yes, it looks like one to me, as well,' said Jack thoughtfully, regarding the huge hairy spider with some suspicion.

'How long have we got before the bomb goes off?' called Dorothy.

Jack looked at the clock on the bomb as it ticked away. 'About twenty seconds!' he called back. 'Which means I've got to deal with this spider whether it likes it or not.'

He looked around quickly for something in which he could hopefully trap the tarantula, and spotted the shoe box on the table. Swiftly he grabbed the shoe box, opened it, and emptied the eerie growths out of it. Then he strode back to the glass box, slid back the lid, and as the tarantula poised to strike up at him, he clapped the box safely over it, trapping the spider without harming it.

That done he reached into the glass box and pulled out the ticking bomb and examined it swiftly.

'There are six seconds left!' he called urgently. 'Which wire is it that I have to pull out, Dorothy?'

'The blue one!' shouted Dorothy.

'No it isn't! It's the brown one!' contradicted M desperately.

Jack shook his head.

'There are only a green wire and a yellow wire here.'

'The cunning swines!' raged M.

'If you pull out the wrong one it'll blow up!' shouted Dorothy, anxious that Jack didn't do anything suddenly dangerous.

Jack looked at the clock which now showed just three seconds to go before the bomb went off. If he couldn't pull out either of the wires then it left him with only one choice. He pulled back his arm, and then threw the bomb with all the force he could managed into the pool. Then he hurled himself at Elizabeth to protect from the blast, just as the bomb went off underwater, sending a huge fountain of water into the cave.

* * *

At the McLog Research Base, Cynthia, McLog and Robert were frantically working to increase the pumping action of the valve to get the antidote into the loch at a faster rate, when there was a dull thud from the sonar that overrode the sound of the creatures.

'What on earth was that?' said McLog.

'It sounded like an explosion underwater!' said Cynthia.

'Look!' cried Robert excitedly.

The other two turned and followed the direction of his finger, which was pointing at the radar screen. As they watched, the five huge 'blips' changed course, turned, and headed back the way they had come, back towards the open sea.

'Whatever it was it's done the trick!' said the relieved McLog. 'It frightened those creatures and they're heading back out towards the open sea! They've been saved!'

'Yes, but have Jack and the others been saved?' asked Cynthia grimly.

'What do you mean?' asked Robert.

'That underwater explosion came from the direction of the Vixen's cave! We'd better get over there and find out what's happened!'

* * *

When Cynthia, McLog and Robert arrived at that underground lab it was to a sight that looked like a scene from a film about jungle hunters: Jack, Kate and Michael had released Elizabeth but from the ceiling hung two nets containing Dorothy, Edward, M, Angus and Tammy. Everyone was soaked from the fountain of water that had erupted into the cave when the bomb went off under water.

'Watch out for traps, Cynthia!' Jack called as they saw Cynthia, McLog and Robert enter. 'The whole place is full of them.'

Cynthia gave a chuckle.

'Ah the old infra-red beam dodge, eh? Where's the switch?' She strode to a control panel and studied it for a second, then said firmly, 'Yes, this is it.'

And she pulled a lever and there were the sounds of thuds as the steel nets and their occupants crashed to the floor of the cave.

'You might have let us know you were going to do that,' protested M, rubbing his knee where he had fallen.

'Anyway, you'll be glad to know that the antidote is now fully effective and the loch is safe again,' Cynthia announced.

'No more toxic monsters!' added McLog with a smile.

'So long as the Vixen didn't get away with that stuff,' pointed out Kate.

'Yes,' said Jack thoughtfully. 'I wonder where they are now?'

In fact at that very moment the Vixen and Jose Cuervo were still chasing around the submarine, Cuervo running away from the tarantula in terror, and the Vixen doing her best to catch it.

'Aarghh!' yelled Cuervo, and he jumped up on the control panel, treading on all the buttons, including the emergency 'flood and sumberge' button. The next second the submarine was filled with the sound of alarm sirens and flashing red lights, and water began to pour through the hatches.

'You idiot!' raged the Vixen.

At the cave, Edward and Elizabeth went to Kate and Michael and put their arms around them, glad to be safely reunited with their children again.

'Don't worry,' said Elizabeth. 'The main thing is that we're all safe.'

'And I suggest we leave catching the Vixen and Cuervo to the authorities,' said Jack.

'That's us!' cried Dorothy enthusiastically. 'Will do Jack!' And she nudged M painfully in the ribs. 'Right, sir?'

'And now,' announced Jack, 'I think after all this excitement, we could all do with a holiday. Somewhere nice and peaceful and away from it all.'

Inside the cave all heads nodded in fervent agreement, the memories of the Vixen and Cuervo still fresh in their minds.

'With no villains and no pollution!' added Kate.

'Right,' nodded Jack. 'Anyone fancy going to Antarctica?'

Other great reads ✦ *from* **Red Fox**

Further Red Fox titles that you might enjoy reading are listed on the following pages. They are available in bookshops or they can be ordered directly from us.

If you would like to order books, please send this form and the money due to:

ARROW BOOKS, BOOKSERVICE BY POST, PO BOX 29, DOUGLAS, ISLE OF MAN, BRITISH ISLES. Please enclose a cheque or postal order made out to Arrow Books Ltd for the amount due, plus 30p per book for postage and packing to a maximum of £3.00, both for orders within the UK. For customers outside the UK, please allow 35p per book.

NAME _____

ADDRESS _____

_____

Please print clearly.

Whilst every effort is made to keep prices low, it is sometimes necessary to increase cover prices at short notice. If you are ordering books by post, to save delay it is advisable to phone to confirm the correct price. The number to ring is THE SALES DEPARTMENT 071 (if outside London) 973 9700.

Other great reads from **Red Fox**

THE SNIFF STORIES Ian Whybrow

Things just keep happening to Ben Moore. It's dead hard avoiding disaster when you've got to keep your street cred with your mates *and* cope with a family of oddballs at the same time. There's his appalling 2½ year old sister, his scatty parents who are into healthy eating and animal rights and, worse than all of these, there's Sniff! If only Ben could just get on with his scientific experiments and his attempt at a world beating *Swampbeast* score . . . but there's no chance of that while chaos is just around the corner.

ISBN 0 09 9750406 £2.50

J.B. SUPERSLEUTH Joan Davenport

James Bond is a small thirteen-year-old with spots and spectacles. But with a name like that, how can he help being a supersleuth?

It all started when James and 'Polly' (Paul) Perkins spotted a teacher's stolen car. After that, more and more mysteries needed solving. With the case of the Arabian prince, the Murdered Model, the Bonfire Night Murder and the Lost Umbrella, JB's reputation at Moorside Comprehensive soars.

But some of the cases aren't quite what they seem . . .

ISBN 0 09 9717808 £1.99

Other great reads *from* **Red Fox**

Adventure Stories from Enid Blyton

THE ADVENTUROUS FOUR

A trip in a Scottish fishing boat turns into the adventure of a lifetime for Mary and Jill, their brother Tom and their friend Andy, when they are wrecked off a deserted island and stumble across an amazing secret. A thrilling adventure for readers from eight to twelve.

ISBN 0 09 9477009   £2.50

THE ADVENTUROUS FOUR AGAIN

'I don't expect we'll have any adventures *this* time,' says Tom, as he and sisters Mary and Jill arrive for another holiday. But Tom couldn't be more mistaken, for when the children sail along the coast to explore the Cliff of Birds with Andy the fisher boy, they discover much more than they bargained for . . .

ISBN 0 09 9477106   £2.50

COME TO THE CIRCUS

When Fenella's Aunt Jane decides to get married and live in Canada, Fenella is rather upset. And when she finds out that she is to be packed off to live with her aunt and uncle at Mr Crack's circus, she is horrified. How will she ever feel at home there when she is so scared of animals?

ISBN 0 09 937590 7   £1.75

Other great reads from **Red Fox**

The latest and funniest joke books are from Red Fox!

THE OZONE FRIENDLY JOKE BOOK
Kim Harris, Chris Langham, Robert Lee,
Richard Turner

What's green and highly dangerous?
How do you start a row between conservationists?
What's green and can't be rubbed out?

Green jokes for green people (non-greens will be pea-green when they see how hard you're laughing), bags and bags of them (biodegradable of course).

All the jokes in this book are printed on environmentally friendly paper and every copy you buy will help GREENPEACE save our planet.

* David Bellamy with a machine gun.
* Pour oil on troubled waters.
* The Indelible hulk.

ISBN 0 09 973190 8   £1.99

THE HAUNTED HOUSE JOKE BOOK
John Hegarty

There are skeletons in the scullery . . .
Beasties in the bath . . .
There are spooks in the sitting room
And jokes to make you laugh . . .

Search your home and see if we are right. Then come back, sit down and shudder to the hauntingly funny and eerily rib-rattling jokes in this book.

ISBN 0 09 9621509   £1.99

Other great reads from **Red Fox**

Discover the wide range of exciting activity books from Red Fox

THE PAINT AND PRINT FUN BOOK
Steve and Megumi Biddle

Would you like to make a glittering bird? A colourful tiger? A stained-glass window? Or an old treasure map? Well, all you need are ordinary materials like vegetables, tinfoil, paper doilies, even your own fingers to make all kinds of amazing things—without too much mess.

Follow Steve and Megumi's step-by-step instructions and clear diagrams and you can make all kinds of professional designs—to hang on your wall or give to your friends.

ISBN 0 09 9644606   £2.50

CRAZY KITES   Peter Eldin

This book is a terrific introduction to the art of flying kites. There are lots of easy-to-assemble, different kites to make, from the basic flat kite to the Chinese dragon and the book also gives you clear instructions on launching, flying and landing. Kite flying is fun. Help yourself to a soaring good time.

ISBN 0 09 964550 5   £2.50

Other great reads from **Red Fox**

Discover the exciting Lenny and Jake adventure series by Hazel Townson!

Lenny Hargreaves wants to be a magician some day, so he's always practising magic tricks. He takes this very seriously, but his friend Jake Allen tends to scoff because he knows the tricks will probably go wrong. All the same, Lenny usually manages to round off one of the exciting and amazing adventures that they keep getting involved in with a trick that solves the problem.

The books in the series are:

The Great Ice Cream Crime
ISBN 0 09 976000 2
£1.99

The Siege of Cobb Street School
ISBN 0 09 975980 2
£1.99

The Vanishing Gran
ISBN 0 09 935480 2
£1.50

Haunted Ivy
ISBN 09 941320 5
£1.99

The Crimson Crescent
ISBN 09 952110 5
£1.50

The Staggering Snowman
ISBN 0 09956820 9
£1.50

Fireworks Galore
ISBN 09 965540 3
£1.99

The Vanishing Gran
ISBN 09 935480 2
£1.50

And the latest story—

Walnut Whirl
Lenny and Jake are being followed by a stranger. Is he a spy trying to recover the microfilm in the walnut shell Lenny has discovered in his pocket? The chase overtakes a school outing to an Elizabethan mansion and there are many hilarious adventures before the truth is finally revealed.

ISBN 0 09 973380 3 £1.99